12/07

DRAGON AND SOLDIER

Dragonback (Starscape Books)
Book 1: Dragon and Thief ★
Book 2: Dragon and Soldier ★

The Blackcollar
A Coming of Age
Cobra
Spinneret
Cobra Strike
Cascade Point and Other Stories
The Backlash Mission
Triplet
Cobra Bargain
Time Bomb and Zahndry Others
Deadman Switch
Warhorse
Cobras Two (omnibus)

Star Wars: Heir to the Empire
Star Wars: Dark Force Rising
Star Wars: The Last Command

Conqueror's Pride
Conqueror's Heritage
Conqueror's Legacy

The Hand of Thrawn
Book 1: Specter of the Past
Book 2: Vision of the Future

The Icarus Hunt
Angelmass ★
Manta's Gift ★

★Denotes a Tor Book

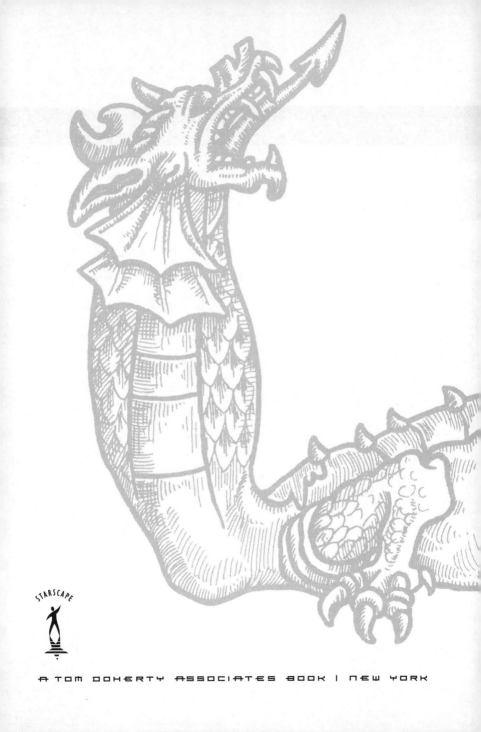

STARSCAPE

A TOM DOHERTY ASSOCIATES BOOK | NEW YORK

DRAGON AND SOLDIER

THE SECOND DRAGONBACK ADVENTURE

TIMOTHY ZAHN

DRAGON AND SOLDIER: THE SECOND DRAGONBACK ADVENTURE

Copyright © 2004 by Timothy Zahn

Edited by James Frenkel

A Starscape Book
Published by Tom Doherty Associates, LLC
175 Fifth Avenue
New York, NY 10010

www.starscape.com

ISBN 0-765-30125-3
EAN 978-0765-30125-3

First Edition: June 2004

Printed in the United States of America

0   9   8   7   6   5   4   3   2   1

For Sable—
who has taught me
what it means to be a symbiont

DRAGON AND SOLDIER

The screams of the dying K'da and Shontine in the Havenseeker's *engine room were growing louder. Draycos tried to shut out the sounds—tried to cover his pointed ears with his paws. But nothing helped.*

He could see them now, back there in the engine room. Which was odd, because Draycos himself was up in the Havenseeker's *control complex, all the way at the other end of the ship. He could see outside through the navigation bubble as the unfamiliar enemy ships sent the all too familiar violet beams of the Death twisting and sweeping across the* Havenseeker's *hull. The Death was coming closer to him . . . closer . . . closer . . .*

With a jerk that sent his claws scratching across the soft plastic coating of the floor beneath him, Draycos woke up.

"Bad dream?" a soft voice came from across the room.

Draycos blinked his eyes, clearing away the last images of the nightmare. The room was mostly dark, but there was enough light for him to see the narrow cot built into the wall at the other end of the small cabin. His new companion, Jack Morgan, was propped up on one elbow, his hair sticking out in a dozen different directions. "Yes," Draycos told him. "I apologize for waking you."

" 'S okay," Jack said, yawning. He ran a hand through his hair without making any noticeable improvement in the mess. "I'm just glad you weren't on my back when you started twitching. What was it this time?"

"The same," Draycos said, the tip of his tail curving into a K'da frown. Odd; he *had* started out the sleep period pressed against Jack's back in his two-dimensional form. When had he jumped off and become fully three-dimensional again? During the terrible dream? "I saw again the destruction of our advance team."

"I don't suppose you happened to notice any markings on those Djinn-90 pursuit fighters this time," Uncle Virge put in.

Draycos glared over at the monitor camera. Uncle Virge was the *Essenay*'s computer, with an artificial personality designed by Jack's late Uncle Virgil. A personality, Draycos had discovered, that often seemed to go out of its way to be irritating. "No, I did not see any markings," he told the computer stiffly. "I saw no markings when they first attacked our ships. I do not expect to see any now that I am merely dreaming of them, either."

"Okay, okay, keep your scales on," Uncle Virge said in a huffy tone. "You're the one who's so hot to track down these pirates or smugglers or whoever."

"They were mercenaries," Draycos said firmly. "Military units of some sort. I have told you that before."

"Yeah," Uncle Virge said. "Whatever."

"And it's not just Draycos who wants to find them, Uncle Virge," Jack said. "I do, too."

"Then let's get serious about it," Uncle Virge said. "Face

it, Jack lad; we simply haven't got the resources for this kind of nickel-in-Nevada search. Not even with our noble K'da poet-warrior standing brave and true at our side. Watching us do all the work."

"We have only just begun our task," Draycos reminded him, ignoring the implied insult. Uncle Virge had made it abundantly clear that he didn't think much of the K'da warrior ethic and its strict emphasis on doing what was right, whatever such actions might cost. He considered such behavior to be impractical, a waste of effort, and fundamentally stupid.

"We've been chasing data for ten days and have come up dry and poor each time," Uncle Virge countered. "I vote we chuck the whole thing and drop it into StarForce's lap where it belongs."

"We cannot do that," Draycos insisted. "Until we know who was responsible for the attack, I cannot risk revealing myself to anyone else. The lives of my people depend on it."

"Oh, come *on,*" Uncle Virge said, and Draycos could almost see a scowling human face behind that voice. "It wasn't StarForce that attacked your ships. The Internos government doesn't go in for genocide."

"Yet someone in StarForce or the Internos may have made a private arrangement without official consent," Draycos pointed out. "I cannot take that risk. We must do this ourselves."

"And what if we can't?" Uncle Virge shot back. "In case you hadn't noticed, friend, the Orion Arm covers a lot of territory. We are one very small frog in one very big pond. Maybe the whole thing makes for a great heroic poem, but we could search from here till geepsday and still not come up with anything."

"What we need is a break," Jack muttered. "Just one. Something to point us in the right direction."

"Don't you think I want that, too, lad?" Uncle Virge asked, his tone suddenly turning earnest and soothing.

Draycos felt his crest stiffen with frustration. In point of fact, Uncle Virge *didn't* want a break. Uncle Virge wanted Jack to turn his back on Draycos, and on the millions of K'da and Shontine refugees who were even now fleeing to the Orion Arm from the threat of the Valahgua and their unstoppable Death weapon.

Uncle Virge, in short, wanted Jack Morgan to go back to the simple day-to-day business of looking out for Jack Morgan.

But he didn't dare point that out. Jack's Uncle Virgil had been a criminal, a con artist and thief, a man who had spent his entire life thinking only of himself. He'd programmed that same self-centered viewpoint into his computerized alter ego before he'd died, and he'd done his best to hammer it into Jack, as well.

Jack had a good heart. Draycos could tell that much. But the boy was only fourteen, and this was an awesome task that Draycos had laid before him.

And even a good heart required training and discipline. Draycos had had only a month to work with him, while Uncle Virgil and the computer had had the past eleven years. If Draycos pushed too hard, the boy might well back away onto the path of long habit.

Besides which, down deep, Draycos had to concede that

Uncle Virge wasn't being entirely unfair. With the lives of his people at stake, Draycos perhaps *was* pushing a little too hard.

But what else could he do?

"I know you want this to work, Draycos," Jack said, running his fingers through his hair again, still without improving the mess. "But face it. This approach just isn't working."

"I agree," Uncle Virge said. "And frankly, I can't see how it ever will. There are just too many Djinn-90s flying around the Orion Arm for us to hunt down the records of all of them. More to the point, there are too many that have changed hands under, shall we way, unofficial circumstances. No matter how many manufacturing records or registration listings we dig up, we still won't have them all."

"Then we need a different approach," Jack concluded. "Draycos, you seem convinced they were mercenaries. How come?"

"I saw them function in battle," Draycos reminded him, the tip of his tail making slow circles as he studied Jack's face in the dim light. The boy's expression was tense, as if he was screwing up his courage toward an unpleasant decision he didn't want to make.

But if that decision was to back away, this was an odd way of leading up to it. "Twice, in fact, both in their attack on our ships and later during our escape from the planet," he went on. "Their maneuvering and tactics were quite professional."

"Doesn't mean they're necessarily soldiers for hire," Uncle Virge argued, his voice gone suddenly cautious. Perhaps he'd picked up on Jack's expression, too. "Maybe they're someone's official military. Maybe some planet has made a deal with your Valahgua enemies."

"An official military would have had backup forces ready," Draycos pointed out. "Our escape would have been far more difficult than it was."

Uncle Virge sniffed. "So maybe they're a stupid military. What's your point, Jack lad?"

"My point is that mercenary groups probably keep close tabs on each other," Jack said slowly. "Including what kinds of pursuit fighters all the other guys have. You think?"

"I suppose," Uncle Virge said. "But I can tell you right now that getting hold of encrypted mercenary files is going to be a lot trickier than pulling up Djinnrabi Aerospace Corporation manufacturing records. I thought we were trying to make this job easier, not harder."

"We're trying to make it work any way we can," Jack said. He paused, and Draycos could see him brace himself. "And you're right. The only way to get merc records will be from the inside."

"You must be joking," Uncle Virge said, his voice sounding like he'd suddenly been hit with a small tree. "Come *on,* Jack lad. Jump up and say 'surprise,' and let's get on with our plans."

"What, you think I can't do it?" Jack snapped. "Fourteen-year-old kids are indentured to mercenary groups all the time."

"And you know what happens to them?" Uncle Virge countered harshly. "They get sent off to war."

Jack seemed to shrink a little in his nightshirt. "I'll be all right," he said, sounding like he was trying to convince himself of that. "There aren't any big wars going on anywhere right now."

"Mercenaries don't hire teenagers just to polish their boots," Uncle Virge insisted. "And you can get just as dead from a little war as you can from a big one."

"I'll be all right." Jack peered across the cabin at Draycos. "Draycos? You're a soldier. You tell him."

"Yes, tell him, Draycos," Uncle Virge demanded, an almost frantic undertone to his voice now. Small wonder: as a computer, even a computer that controlled the entire ship, he had no physical power to make Jack do anything he didn't want to do. All Uncle Virge could do was persuade.

And unless Draycos was misjudging Jack's expression, the boy's mind was already made up. Not enthusiastically, but definitely made up. "Tell him what it takes to be a soldier," Uncle Virge went on. "Tell him how old *you* were when you went into your first battle. Tell him how many friends you've seen die."

"In many ways, Uncle Virge is right, Jack," Draycos said. "If it were for anything less important I would agree that this was too dangerous for you. *But.*"

"Don't say it," Uncle Virge warned. "Draycos, don't say it."

"I am sorry, but I must," Draycos said. "The fate of the K'da and Shontine races hang by the edge of a single torn scale. With only five months remaining until they arrive, we have no choice but to take chances."

"Maybe *you* have to take chances," Uncle Virge snapped. "But why does Jack have to?"

"Because I promised to help him," Jack said.

"And I will be with him the whole way," Draycos added.

"Wonderful," Uncle Virge said sarcastically. "A golden dragon plastered flat across his back. That gives me *such* confidence."

"Oh, stop being melodramatic," Jack scolded. "It's not like I'm making a career of this. I'll get in, scam their computer and find their records on their competitors, and get back out. Piece of fudge cake."

"Unless they catch you," Uncle Virge said. "You ever think of *that*?"

"I'll be fine," Jack insisted. "Anyway, like Draycos says, he'll be with me the whole way."

Uncle Virge didn't answer. "So that's settled," Jack said, flopping back flat onto the cot again. "If you want to be helpful, you can find us a good merc group to try. Something not too big, but with jobs all across the Orion Arm. We don't want someone who just works locally. And make sure it's someone who hires a lot of kids my age—"

"And isn't too fussy about who they take," Uncle Virge cut him off grudgingly. "Yes, yes, I know what to look for."

"And when you find one, put us on ECHO for their nearest recruitment center," Jack added. "No point in wasting time."

"No, of course not," Uncle Virge muttered. "Good night, Jack lad."

Jack pushed himself up off the cot again. "Draycos, you getting back aboard? You're going to need to do it sometime before morning anyway."

Draycos focused on the clock built into the wall beside Jack's cot. Yes; even if he had broken contact with the boy just before his dream began, he would still come close to his limit before the sleep period was over. A K'da could only go six hours before he needed to return to two-dimensional form against a host's body. If he stayed away longer than that, he would still become two-dimensional, and ripple away into death.

But he had time. And his body always gave him plenty of warning. "I will join you later," he decided, standing up and stretching all four legs. "I believe I will go watch Uncle Virge work through the mercenary information."

"Going to be some awfully big words there," Uncle Virge warned sourly. "You may not be up to third-grade reading level yet."

"I can use the practice," Draycos assured him calmly. After only ten days of study, he had already made good headway in learning to read the humans' written language. His progress had pleased him, amazed Jack, and no doubt irritated Uncle Virge. A worthwhile accomplishment on all three counts. "Rest well, Jack," he added as he headed across the cabin.

"Sure," Jack said, already starting to sound sleepy again. "By the way, how old *were* you when you were in your first battle?"

Draycos paused in the doorway. "I was younger than you," he said quietly, turning his long neck to look around behind him. "And the K'da and Shontine lost that battle."

"Younger than me," Jack repeated, his voice sounding odd. "You had loose rules, didn't you?"

"We were fighting for our survival," Draycos reminded him. "We still are."

Jack didn't say anything. For a wonder, neither did Uncle Virge.

CHAPTER 2

The planet Carrion was, in Jack's opinion, a very appropriately named world.

Or so it seemed as he paid the taxi driver and joined the stream of pedestrians hurrying along the wide sidewalks. Even just glancing around, he could spot the uniforms of a half dozen different mercenary groups among the crowds. The men and women inside the uniforms were rough-looking types, all of them with small areas of empty space around them as they strode along. Like arrogant vultures gathered to feed on their prey, he thought darkly, with the ordinary citizens trying to keep as far away from them as possible.

Or maybe he was imagining the citizens' reaction. Maybe he was just projecting his own feelings onto the people around him.

What in the world was he doing here, anyway?

"Is that it ahead?" Draycos murmured from his right shoulder.

Jack made a face as he focused on the plain white building half a block down the street ahead of them. "That's it," he confirmed. "The main Carrion recruitment office of the Whinyard's Edge."

"A whinyard was a Scottish name for a dagger or short sword," Uncle Virge put in from the comm clip fastened to Jack's left collar. "It dates back to—"

"Thank you, Professor," Jack cut him off. The last thing he was in the mood for right now was a history lesson. "Unless you've got something useful to say, everyone just shut up. Okay?"

"Have the young people from the spaceport arrived yet?" Draycos asked.

"I don't see them," Jack said, craning his neck to try to look over the crowd and slowing down a little. He didn't want to reach the recruitment office before the group he and Draycos had spotted being gathered together at the spaceport. The idea was to blend in with them when they went in to sign their enlistment papers, not to be the one leading the charge. "They were probably getting them here by bus. Busses always take longer than cabs."

"A bus also implies they're expected, Jack lad," Uncle Virge warned. "That means the Whinyard's Edge will know how many of them there are supposed to be."

"Maybe," Jack said. "I can handle that."

"It's not too late to back out," Uncle Virge went on. "We could try to put together enough money to simply buy the information we need from them."

"And if they refuse, it'll just put them on their guard," Jack pointed out. "Hang on a second."

Ahead, a sleek bus pulled to the curb in front of the white building. "Okay, they're here," Jack confirmed as a boy his age got rather hesitantly off the bus. "I'm shutting down," he added, reaching for the comm clip. "Wish me luck."

There was an electronic sigh. "Good luck," Uncle Virge said.

Jack clicked off the clip, unfastened it, and slipped it into his pocket. The first kids off the bus had gathered into a little group by the curb, hanging back instead of going directly into the building. Either they were nervous, or else they were waiting for someone who was still behind them.

"You have not yet explained this indenture process," Draycos said from his shoulder.

"It's sort of like an apprenticeship," Jack said. An adult was getting off now, a woman wearing a Whinyard's Edge uniform. Not only were they expected, but the mercenaries had even sent a babysitter to the spaceport to herd them in. "Parents hire their kids out to different merc groups, usually for two to five years."

"And what do they receive in exchange?"

"Cash," Jack told him. "Lots of it."

"It is a form of slavery," Draycos declared, his voice dark. "Your people permit this?"

"Not exactly," Jack said. The woman was striding toward the white building, the kids following like scared but obedient ducklings. This was probably the first time most of them had ever been away from home, he suspected. "The Internos government officially condemns it, but there are plenty of human worlds that sort of wink at the whole thing. Mostly the poorer ones where the people don't have any other way to make a living."

"There are always other ways," Draycos insisted. "This is not the behavior of a civilized society."

"No, of course not," Jack soothed. Uncivilized this, uncivilized that—the dragon needed to lighten up a little. Things were the way they were; and like it or not, there wasn't a thing you could do about it.

The universe was a giant mulching machine, Uncle Virgil had often said. If you were smart, you rolled with the gears. If you weren't, you got chewed up by them.

"And there are so very many of them," Draycos murmured, obviously still brooding about it.

"Which is what we want, remember?" Jack reminded him patiently. "Uncle Virge said this was one of only a couple of groups who were hiring lots of kids right now. The more they've got coming in, the easier it'll be for me to slip in and get lost in the crowd."

"I understand the reasoning," Draycos said, a bit tartly. "That does not mean I have to enjoy my part in this."

The last kid had gotten off the bus. "Okay," Jack muttered, taking a deep breath and picking up his pace. "Nice and easy. Here we go."

And as the last boy in line walked through the white building's door, Jack closed the gap and stepped in right behind him.

He found himself in a large reception room with a pair of ornate desks at the far end beneath a huge wood carving of the Whinyard's Edge insignia. The woman who had escorted the teens in from the bus was seated at one of the desks, while an older gray-haired man sat at the other.

Off to either side of the main room, near where Jack had

entered, were a pair of unmarked doorways. One of the doors was slightly ajar, and through it Jack caught a glimpse of the simple desk and filing cabinets of a secretarial work station. On the far back wall, behind the fancy desks and directly beneath the wooden insignia, was a door with a picture of a dagger painted on it and what looked like a motto stenciled around its edge.

The number of teens in the reception room was a surprise. Even huddled together like sheep the way they were, they filled the room all the way to the walls. The bus Jack had seen pull up must have been only the last of a group of them, possibly bringing in new recruits from several different parts of the spaceport. Apparently, the Whinyard's Edge was holding an even bigger recruitment drive than he'd realized.

Briefly, his mind flicked back to his confident statement to Uncle Virge that there were no major wars going on anywhere. He hoped he hadn't been wrong about that.

"Over there," Draycos murmured, just loud enough for Jack to hear over the soft buzz of conversation. The dragon's snout rose slightly from Jack's upper chest beneath his shirt, pointing to the left. "That boy has papers."

"Uh-huh," Jack said. More than just papers: it was an official looking document with a blue-paper backing sheet. A document that Jack himself didn't have.

This was not good.

Carefully, casually, he eased through the crowd and came up behind the boy. "Some place, huh?" he commented.

"Terrific," the other said, his voice trembling slightly. First time away from home, all right.

"Hey, buck up," Jack said, trying for a cheerfully encouraging tone he suddenly wasn't feeling anymore. The paper the boy was holding was an official indenture agreement.

On an official Whinyard's Edge form. With an official Whinyard's Edge signature on the bottom.

And suddenly Jack's plan of simply talking his way inside as part of the group wasn't looking so hot anymore.

"Yeah, right," the boy said. "Just like summer camp. How long you in for?"

"Probably the same as you," Jack improvised, searching the form for the correct number. There was a small bit of weight at his collarbone as Draycos lifted an eye up to look over the boy's shoulder. "Two years, right?"

The boy snorted under his breath. "I guess your folks must not need the money," he said, waving the form up into Jack's face. The name at the top caught Jack's eye: Jommy Randolph. "I'm in for five. Five whole years."

"Put a quark in it," a girl at Jack's other side growled. She was maybe thirteen, with jet-black hair and eyes that were so dark they were almost black, too.

"You talking to me?" Jommy demanded, his voice threatening.

"You see anyone else in here whining about life?" she countered.

"Maybe it's just that no one else gets it," Jommy said, taking a half step toward her. Clearly, he wasn't in the mood for criticism.

The girl stood her ground. "Or maybe it's just that no

one else's glue is melting," she said. "You'd think they were drop-kicking you into prison or something."

"Oh, they're drop-kicking us, all right," Jommy shot back. "I had an uncle once—"

"Quiet back there!" a deep voice snapped from the far end of the room, the words cutting through the buzz.

The buzz instantly evaporated. Grimacing to himself, Jack backed away from Jommy and the girl and started to ease his way to the exit. Uncle Virge had been right; this had been a lousy idea. Time to wave bye-bye and head for the tall grass.

"There is a guard," Draycos whispered.

Jack looked over his shoulder. There was a guard, all right, standing at attention between him and the door. A very big guard, in full uniform, with a very big gun belted at his waist.

So much for a gracious retreat. "I'm open to suggestions," he muttered, turning away from the guard.

"To your left," Draycos said. "The room with the open door."

"Good idea," Jack said, drifting in that direction. The buzz of whispered conversation was starting to come back now, despite the order for silence. Maybe they *all* thought it was going to be like summer camp. "We'll try for a window."

"You will not be going into the room," Draycos said. "I will need five minutes alone. Unfasten your sleeve."

Jack frowned. But he obeyed, unsnapping the cuffs of his leather jacket as he eased toward the slightly open door. Beneath his shirt, he could feel Draycos sliding along his skin, moving as much of his two-dimensional form as he could onto Jack's left arm.

Obviously preparing to spring out the end of that sleeve. Problem was, Jack couldn't see what that would gain them.

He had reached the door now, listening as best he could over the murmurs of the crowd. He hadn't spotted anyone in the room earlier, and he couldn't hear anyone in there now. But that didn't prove anything. They would just have to gamble that the office was indeed empty. "Ready?" he whispered.

Draycos's affirmative was signaled by a light claw-tap on his arm. Jack stepped to the office door, swung his left hand smoothly into the open gap—

And with a sudden brief surge of weight, Draycos went three-dimensional as he leaped out through the end of the sleeve. Jack caught a flicker of gold scales as the dragon dodged out of sight behind the door, and then was gone.

Keeping his movements smooth, Jack dropped his arm back to his side and kept moving. No startled screams came from behind him; the office must have been empty after all.

He continued his apparently aimless wandering along the edge of the crowd, trying to figure out what Draycos had in mind. Was he planning on going out a window and jumping the door guard from behind? Jack had seen the K'da poet-warrior in action, and knew he could pull it off.

But going outside and coming in again would mean showing himself on a busy street. Surely he wouldn't do that. Not unless they were desperate. They weren't *that* desperate yet, were they?

The minutes ticked by. Jack stayed near the back of the crowd, occasionally wandering around some more so that it wouldn't look suspicious when he eventually returned to the office. The guard at the door stayed put, and no golden-scaled dragon suddenly appeared from the doorway behind him.

Slowly, the crowd shrank as the teens were processed and disappeared through the dagger-decorated door. Slowly; but still too fast for Jack's comfort. Already the back of the group had pulled away from the area around Draycos's office. That meant that when Jack went back to retrieve his companion, he would no longer have people standing all around to help mask his movements.

Too bad he hadn't known any of this was coming. Aboard the *Essenay* he had a whole collection of time-delay firecrackers designed for use as diversions. Too late now.

In the old days, Uncle Virgil would have been right there beside him, ready to jump in with an improvised change of plans. But then, in the old days he and Uncle Virgil never had any life-and-death situations hanging over them. They never had the fate of two entire species depending on whether they could pull off some scam or theft. All they'd ever had to worry about was closing a deal, or popping a safe, and then getting out before the cops arrived.

How had he gotten himself into this, anyway?

Jack looked around the room at the other kids, feeling his throat tighten. He knew the facts of how this had happened, of course. How he'd bumped into the ambushed K'da/Shontine ship and found Draycos dying amid the wreckage. How they'd escaped from the people who had attacked Draycos's people, and gone on to solve the frame-up that Jack had been hiding from in the first place.

But in the old days, that would have been the end of it. Uncle Virgil would have calmly and cheerfully gone back on his promise to help Draycos find the people who had attacked him. He would have kicked the dragon out to fend for himself, and he and Jack would have flown off to get on with their lives. Nice, neat, and very simple.

So what *was* Jack doing here? Draycos had already said he wouldn't force himself on a host who didn't want him. Why didn't Jack simply dump him on StarForce like Uncle Virge wanted?

Was it because he'd made Draycos a promise? Could this K'da warrior-ethic thing actually be starting to rub off on him?

He hoped not. He desperately hoped not. It was all well and good for Draycos to be strong and noble—he was an adult, and he'd been trained for that sort of thing. But Jack was only fourteen years old, and very much alone in the universe. There was no way he could deal with the complications a K'da warrior ethic demanded of a person.

More to the point, he didn't *want* to deal with them. Life was hard enough without making it any harder.

Draycos's five minutes were up. As casually as he could manage, Jack strolled back to the office door.

He reached it and turned to lean his back against the jamb, gazing blankly out at the crowd. As he did so, he dropped one hand to his side and scratched gently against the wood.

From inside came an answering scratch. Good; Draycos was ready. Now if only the guard over by the exit could conveniently be looking somewhere else.

He wasn't. He was staring straight at Jack, a very unpleasant look on his face.

Jack let his eyes drift away, trying hard to look as innocent as a newborn kitten. It looked like he was going to have to do this right under the guard's nose.

Okay. No problem. Bracing himself, hoping the dragon really *was* ready, he turned around suddenly as if startled and leaned his head slightly into the office. As he did so, his right hand dipped into the open doorway—

The sudden weight on his palm nearly toppled him over onto his nose. Fortunately, it disappeared almost immediately as Draycos flattened himself into two-dimensional form onto Jack's skin and slithered up his arm beneath his shirt. Jack regained his balance and turned back around.

And was suddenly hauled nearly off his feet by the front of his jacket.

The door guard was no longer at the door. He was standing right in front of Jack, a fistful of Jack's jacket clutched in his hand.

And the unpleasant expression had become downright ugly.

CHAPTER 3

"What do you think you're doing?" the guard demanded. His voice was surprisingly quiet, almost civilized. It made the glare on his face even scarier by contrast.

"I thought I heard something," Jack said, trying to sound nervous and flustered. It didn't take much acting. "Like there was someone in there."

"So?" the guard demanded. He turned his hand a little, twisting the wad of jacket in his grip. "What's it to you?"

Jack would have thought the conversation was quiet enough to have escaped notice. He was wrong. "Sergeant?" the deep voice called from the other end of the room.

"Got a candidate here for an Intelligence assignment, sir," the guard called back. "Caught his nose where it wasn't supposed to be."

"Bring him," the voice ordered.

The guard let go of the front of Jack's coat, shifting his grip to the back collar, and quick-marched him across the room. The crowd of teens magically parted in front of them, leaving a clear path to the two desks.

Jack hadn't yet had a good look at the man at the second desk. Now, as the guard shoved him forward, he saw that the other was younger than he'd first thought. He was probably no older than his late twenties, though the gray hair made him seem twice that age. His expression was cool and thoughtful as he watched Jack approach. His collar insignia was that of a lieutenant; the small nameplate over his right shirt pocket read BASHT.

He waited until Jack had been deposited directly in front of him before speaking again. "Name?" he asked.

"Jack Montana," Jack said, pulling out the fake ID he'd put together aboard the *Essenay*. "From Cartier," he added, holding it out.

Lieutenant Basht made no move to take the card. "What was the commotion about?"

Jack swallowed. "I thought I heard a noise in there," he said. "I just looked in, just for a second."

"He didn't just look in," the guard insisted. "He had his hand inside the door—"

Basht silenced him with a glance. "You always investigate noises in places you have no business being?" he asked.

"It's my uncle," Jack explained hesitantly. "He told me once about a merc group that liked to hide soldiers in their recruitment centers. They'd pop out suddenly and start shooting."

A murmur of reaction went through the teens behind him. Basht's face didn't even twitch. "No reputable mercenary organization would ever do a thing like that," he said in a precise voice. "We don't waste people for no good reason."

"They figured anyone who was fast enough to duck had

what they were looking for," Jack said, making his voice tremble a little. "The rest weren't worth the effort to train."

For a long moment Basht stared up at him in silence. Jack dropped into what Uncle Virgil used to call "little-boy mode": making eye contact with the man, cringing and letting his gaze drop away, then forcing himself to look at him again. It was supposed to make Jack look all innocent and scared, and to hopefully squeeze a little pity out of the opposition.

Problem was, he wasn't sure that was the effect he wanted here. It might get him off this particular hook, but it might also get him booted straight out the door behind him. That wasn't exactly what he and Draycos had had in mind.

"So," Basht said at last. "You looked in."

Jack nodded. "Yes, sir."

"*Just* looked in?"

"Yes, sir."

"Really," Basht said, his voice suddenly the temperature of a walk-in freezer. "Then how do you explain that your papers are halfway *into* the office?"

Jack blinked. "Excuse me?"

Basht pointed past Jack's side. "Those *are* your papers, aren't they?"

Jack turned around. Lying on the floor partway into the office, half visible from where he stood, was a neatly folded set of papers with a blue backing. The same blue backing, he realized, that had been on Jommy Randolph's indenture agreement.

Only then did he finally catch on. An office, a secretary's

work station, neat stacks of blank Whinyard's Edge forms conveniently lying around . . .

And a clever and resourceful K'da poet-warrior.

Score one for the dragon.

"I don't know," he said, fumbling at his inside jacket pockets as if looking for something that should have been there. "I guess . . . I guess so."

Basht's eyes flicked to the side. "You," he said to one of the teens. "Go get it."

The teen hurried to the office and returned with the blue-backed paper. "Jack Montana," Basht read aloud. He frowned as he looked down the sheet. "Who filled this out, your baby sister?"

"My parents didn't have much school-learning," Jack improvised. Draycos's reading skills were improving rapidly, but his penmanship still needed a lot of work.

"Let's hope yours was better," Basht said. "Are you satisfied yet that we aren't going to shoot you in the back?"

Jack swallowed again. "Yes, sir. I'm . . . I guess I was just . . ."

"Don't make excuses, Montana," Basht said coldly. "Edgemen do their jobs right and take the credit, or they do them wrong and take the consequences. There's no middle ground. Is that clear?"

Jack straightened up. "Yes, sir."

Basht watched him a few seconds longer, as if determined to make him wiggle as much as possible. Then he jerked his head fractionally toward the door behind him. "Go get your gear," he ordered.

For the first time in several minutes, Jack took a clear breath. "Yes, sir."

Behind the door a short corridor branched off in two directions, the doors marked by the interstellar symbols for male and female. Jack took the door to the right, and found himself in a large chamber filled with locker-room–style changing benches. Along one wall was a long supply counter with a dozen men working behind it. At the far end was a stack of footlockers. Fifty or so of Jack's fellow recruits were already gathered around the changing benches, in various stages of changing from their street clothes into light gray Whinyard's Edge uniforms.

"Welcome to paradise," Jack murmured to himself, and joined the line at the counter.

The supply men were very efficient. In a few dizzying minutes Jack had had a quick blood sample drawn and a full-body scan taken, been issued a dress uniform, boots, and four sets of fatigues, collected a field kit and operations manual, and had been pointed toward the stack of footlockers. Finding an open space at a bench along the back wall, he started to change.

He had stripped to his underwear, and was shaking out the uniform shirt, when he suddenly realized all conversation in the room had stopped.

He turned around. The whole room was standing frozen in place, from the new teenage recruits to the supply men behind their counter. All of them staring at him.

No. Not at him. At the K'da warrior wrapped around his body.

Jack felt suddenly sick. He'd gotten so used to having Draycos riding his skin that he'd completely forgotten about him. With his mind still focused on his near-miss out in the reception room, he hadn't even stopped to think about what he was doing.

Now, with a single act of unthinking carelessness, he'd ruined everything. Draycos's secret was gone, announced to the whole Orion Arm from a grubby mercenary changing room.

And as Draycos's secret crumbled, so did any hope for his people. Their enemies would silence him with ease now; and in five months the K'da and Shontine refugee fleet would arrive at their new home only to find a deadly ambush waiting.

They were dead. They were all dead. And Jack was the one who had killed them.

"Wow!" the kid beside Jack said, his eyes wide.

Jack focused on him. "You like my dragon?" he asked. The words came out with difficulty, his voice sounding in his ears like it was coming from deep inside a well.

"It's cool," the kid said. "I've never seen a tattoo that big before."

For a long heartbeat Jack just stared at him. And then, as abruptly as it had crumbled to dust, the whole thing uncrumbled itself back together again.

He'd gotten used to Draycos riding his skin, all right. So

used to it that he'd also forgotten what the K'da looked like stretched out back there. "Biggest one in the Orion Arm," he bragged. His voice sounded just fine now. "At least, that's what the guy said."

The kid shook his head in wonder, leaning forward for a better look. "How long did it take him to do it?" he asked.

"Couple of months," Jack improvised, hoping that wasn't a ridiculous number. He didn't have the faintest idea how long it took to put on a tattoo. "He did part of it every day until it was done."

The kid shook his head again. "Cool."

Jack frowned at him. The kid was a good head shorter than he was, with a wide, round face and ears that stuck out to the sides. Like a hot-air balloon with twin air scoops attached, he decided. "I'm Jack Montana," he introduced himself.

"Rogan Mbusu," the other said.

"Uh-huh," Jack said. "How old are you, Rogan?"

The kid drew back a little. "I'm fourteen," he said, a little defiantly. "I'll be fifteen on my next birthday."

"Yeah, that's the way birthdays usually work," Jack said, frowning. No way the kid was fourteen. Even twelve would be pushing it. "Fourteen, huh?"

Rogan's eyes drifted away. "Sure," he said. Turning back to his own section of the bench, he resumed changing into his new uniform.

Jack looked back around the room. A few of the boys

were still staring at him, but most had had their fill of the show and were going about their business again. Turning his back to them, Jack did likewise.

A few minutes later he was finished. Folding his civilian clothing into the footlocker, he pulled the "dog-collar" wristband from its pouch inside the lid and closed it, making sure all the locks were fastened. He slid the wristband around his right wrist and headed toward the line of uniformed kids at the wide exit door. The footlocker, following the signal from his wristband, rolled along at his side like an obedient puppy.

On the far side of the exit door was another supply counter. There Jack picked up a combat vest with a dozen pockets, a condensation canteen, a shirt nameplate, and the results of the medical scan they'd done on him at the other end of the line.

Last of all, he was issued his weapons.

"Moray pistol and Gompers flash rifle," the supply man identified the handgun and snub-nosed rifle as he slid them across the counter. His voice had the bored tone of someone who's been saying the same thing once a minute since breakfast. "Holster's in the side trouser pocket—pick either left- or right-handed. Rifle goes over the shoulder, barrel down, grip back."

"Uh—" Jack frowned at the guns as he picked them up. They were a lot heavier than he'd expected. "Grip how?"

"Come on, come on, move along," the man snapped, already pushing the next recruit's weapons across the counter.

Fumbling the guns into an awkward grip, Jack moved away. At the end of the room ahead was one final door, with glimpses of daylight shining through each time one of the new recruits went out. He looped the rifle sling over one shoulder, just to get it out of the way, and slid his hand into his right-hand pocket. The man had said there was a holster somewhere in there?

"It goes like this," a girl's voice said from behind him.

Jack turned, to see the dark-eyed girl who'd had the brief run-in earlier with Jommy Randolph. "What?" he asked.

"I said it goes like this," she repeated. She patted her right hip, where her Moray was already nestled in its holster. "You pull the tab and it folds out into shape."

"Oh." Jack located the tab and pulled. Sure enough, the holster folded out. "Right. Thanks."

"The rifle goes like this," she added, looping the sling over her right shoulder with the gun pointed down and the top of the barrel facing forward. "This way you can just grab the grip and swing it up on its strap into firing position." She demonstrated. "See?"

"Yeah," Jack said, tucking his Moray away and redoing the rifle. Gingerly, he swung it up. "Yeah, I see."

"Don't worry, it won't bite," she assured him, her face somewhere between contempt and amusement. "See the red spirals along the barrels? These are candy canes."

"They're what?"

"Candy canes. Non-functional guns."

Jack frowned down at his rifle. "What are they giving us non-functional guns for?"

She shrugged. "Get us used to carrying the weight, I suppose."

"But why not use real ones?" Jack persisted. "They're going to give us those before we go into the field anyway, aren't they?"

She snorted. "If you want to get on a crowded transport with a hundred farm boys like you who've never seen a gun before *and* who have live ammo, go ahead. Me, I'll stick with Santa's elves and their candy canes."

"I have too seen guns before," Jack insisted irritably. This girl had a genuine knack for rubbing people the wrong way. "Just not this particular type."

"Sure," she said. "Just keep 'em pointed at the ground, okay?" She nodded toward his left hand. "You need help with that, too?"

Jack looked down at the nameplate still in his hand. "I think I can figure that one out for myself, thanks," he growled.

"I'm sure," she said. Her own name plate, he saw, was already neatly pinned over her right shirt pocket. KAYNA, it said. "The name's Montana, right?"

"Yes," Jack said. "Call me Jack."

"Call me Kayna," she said pointedly. She took another look at his face, and her lip twitched. "Or Alison," she added, almost grudgingly.

"Nice to meet you, Alison," Jack said.

"Yeah. Right." She tapped her own name plate. "And remember: If *you* can read it, it's upside down."

She smiled sweetly and moved off, her footlocker rolling along beside her. Muttering under his breath, Jack pinned his nameplate into place and followed.

Maybe Jommy had been right. Maybe this *was* going to be like prison.

CHAPTER 4

Half an hour later, after a lot of jostling and confusion, the new recruits and their luggage were finally aboard the transports.

The seats were hard and narrow, and the teens were squeezed together like slabs of packaged meat. Jammed against the two boys on either side of him, apologizing as his equipment poked into their ribs and wincing as theirs poked into his, Jack had to admit Alison had been right. He was just as glad no one aboard had live ammo.

He tried a few times to strike up conversations, but no one nearby seemed interested in talking. Eventually he gave up the effort and spent the rest of the trip gazing moodily at the seat in front of him. With his comm clip connection to Uncle Virge buried inside his footlocker, and with too many people pressed around for him to risk talking to Draycos, he felt strangely lonely.

It was an hour before they set down in the center of what looked like a random collection of small huts, large prefabricated buildings, and a scattering of tents of various colors and styles. The recruits were herded off their transports and ordered into one of three long barracks buildings nestled under the trees.

Jack had hoped to get a bed near one of the handful of tall, narrow windows, with an eye toward the kind of midnight computer raid he and Draycos were probably going to have to make. But everyone else seemed to want a bunk with a view, too, and he had to settle for a lower bunk pressed up against the washroom wall. It wasn't exactly a prime location, but the washroom had some windows high up in the walls that might do.

The recruits spent the next two hours sitting on their bunks filling out more paperwork. After that, they were taken outside into an open field and taught how to stand at attention, turn precise corners, and march in unison.

Dinner time was a real treat. Jack had heard once that the stronger the army, the more disgusting its food. By that standard, the Whinyard's Edge was a very good army indeed. An early round of muttered complaints was quickly cut off by a large sergeant, who ordered one of the complainers to stand at attention while he verbally took him apart inch by inch. Sergeant Grisko, someone at Jack's table whispered the man's name, rumored to be the meanest of the Edge's drill instructors. After that, everyone ate in silence.

After dinner it was back to the barracks, with orders to study their training manuals. The ten-minute warning sounded at eight-fifty, and at precisely nine o'clock the lights went out. Many of the teens were caught unprepared, and there was a lot of stumbling around and clunking into bunks and each other for the next half hour.

Only then, after the barracks was quiet, did Jack finally have a chance to talk to Draycos.

"So," he whispered, his head half under the blankets to muffle his voice. "This is what it's like to be a soldier, huh?"

"Not precisely," Draycos murmured back. Even in a whisper, his voice sounded odd. "It is similar, though."

Jack craned his neck to try to look down at the dragon's face lying against his shoulder. "You all right?"

For a long moment Draycos was silent. "This is not right," he said. "For children so young to be sold into such a life without cause is not right."

"You said you were younger than this when you became a soldier," Jack reminded him.

"We were in a war for survival," Draycos said. "There is no such reasoning here."

"I suppose not," Jack conceded. "Though I know there are sometimes big fights off on backwater worlds that the rest of us never hear about."

The dragon shook his head. At least that was what it felt like against Jack's skin. "Cornelius Braxton would not approve of this situation."

"Braxton?" Jack echoed, frowning. "How did Braxton get into this?"

"I believe him to be an honorable human," Draycos said. "He would be strongly opposed to children being used for such a purpose."

"Fine, but how did—oh, never mind," Jack said, giving up. Sometimes Draycos's mind wandered off onto the strangest bunny trails. "Just don't forget that he didn't build Braxton Universis into one of the Orion Arm's biggest megacorporations by being Saint Boy Scout. The only reason he was so nice to me was because we did him a big favor. If he had to indenture kids to get something he wanted, I bet he'd do it. He might not like it, but he'd do it."

"Perhaps," Draycos said. "Still, you and I at least should have nothing to fear from him."

"I'm not so sure about that, either," Jack said, thinking back to the glint in Braxton's eye at their last meeting. "I wasn't exactly telling him the whole truth about what happened, you know. I get the feeling people don't tell half-truths to Cornelius Braxton and get away with it. He may not be finished with us yet." He grimaced. "I'd lay odds that Arthur Neverlin isn't finished with us, either."

"Perhaps," Draycos said. "But I would suspect that Neverlin has all he can do right now trying to conceal himself from Braxton."

"Don't you believe it," Jack warned. "Snakes like Neverlin can always find time for a little revenge when someone's double crossed him. Especially when they've double-crossed him as badly as we did."

"A double cross implies there was a legitimate agreement to begin with," Draycos pointed out. "You were blackmailed into assisting him."

"You think that's going to matter to Neverlin?"

"I suppose not," Draycos conceded, his voice thoughtful.

Again, Jack tried to get a look at the dragon's face. "So where exactly are you going with this line of conversation?" he asked. "You suggesting we ask Braxton for help?"

"Certainly not," Draycos said firmly, his mind apparently

finished with wherever it had been wandering. "You know we cannot afford to let anyone know there was a survivor of the Valahgua attack. I have simply been thinking about Braxton today."

"And I'm sure he appreciates it," Jack said. "Can we forget him now and concentrate on the problem at hand?"

"Yes, of course," Draycos said. "What do you wish me to do?"

"First of all, you eat," Jack said, reaching under his bunk to the napkin-wrapped slices of meat he'd managed to smuggle out of the mess hall. "There isn't much here, I'm afraid. I'll try to do better tomorrow."

"I am grateful." Draycos's head rose from Jack's chest, pushing up the blankets.

One by one, Jack fed the meat slices into his open mouth, maneuvering carefully between the sharp teeth. It felt rather like feeding a pet dog, he thought.

He quickly and firmly put the warm-fuzzy image away. Draycos had already made it clear he wasn't anyone's pet. "I can hunt if necessary, as well," the dragon said, still chewing as his head sank flat against Jack's chest again. "What is next?"

"The main computer system is probably in the headquarters," Jack said. "It's a big, three-story gray building through the trees facing the landing area. It had a flag flying in front of it earlier."

"I saw it."

"Good," Jack said. He was never quite sure how much Draycos could see riding his skin that way. "There may be a way to tap into their records from somewhere else, but I'm guessing the HQ is our best bet. And since they probably aren't going to let us just walk in and sift through their files during the day, it's going to have to be at night."

"There will be guard patrols," Draycos pointed out. "As well as alarms."

"Right," Jack agreed. "Nothing we can do about the alarms until we can get a close look at them. But we should at least be able to figure out the patrols."

"Yes," Draycos said. The blankets swelled upward again as the dragon raised his head from Jack's shoulder and poked his snout into the open air. "These windows do not face the proper direction."

"There are some in the washroom that do," Jack said. "High up on the walls. You should be able to see the HQ and most of the area around it from there."

"Good." Draycos rose higher off Jack's skin and stretched his neck, the movement shaking his head completely out of concealment. "Hold your breath."

Frowning, Jack took a deep breath and held it. For perhaps twenty seconds the dragon sat there like a statue, his golden scales seeming to glow in the pale light. Every few seconds his ears would twitch; and then, abruptly, he nodded. "They are all asleep," he said, dropping lightly onto the floor beside Jack's cot. "I will need your watch."

Jack handed it over. "They said reveille would be at four-thirty," he warned the dragon. "Don't pull a Cinderella on me."

"Pardon?"

"Skip it," Jack said, resettling the blankets over his shoulders and rolling onto his side. It had been a long day, and he suddenly realized he was very tired indeed. "Just don't be late. And try not to wake me up when you get home."

CHAPTER 5

Reveille came precisely at four-thirty, a raucous trumpet blare that sent bunks jerking all through the barracks. Thirty seconds later, Sergeant Grisko himself came striding through the door, bellowing for all the greasy maggot-infested sacks of lard to get their hind ends out of bed and stand at attention.

"Sloppy, maggots," he growled when the teens were standing stiffly at the ends of their bunks. "What do you think this is, summer camp? Well, it's not. Who do you think I am, your mother? Well, I'm *not*."

He stomped slowly down the room between the lines, looking each recruit up and down as he went, describing in vivid detail exactly what he thought of them, their parents, their expectations, and their chances of becoming successful soldiers. It was highly intimidating, as it was no doubt meant to be.

At the same time, Jack couldn't help but admire the range of the man's vocabulary. He'd spent a fair amount of time over the years in the company of Uncle Virgil's associates, and he'd always assumed their language was as vile as it got.

Grisko's loud defense of the cooking staff the previous evening had already put him in the same high-level cursing league as those men. Only now did Jack realize how restrained the sergeant's mess hall tirade had actually been.

And this was just the first early-morning wakeup. He wondered how much the man still had in reserve.

He reached Jack . . . and suddenly stopped cold. "What in the name of Cutter's Hind End are *you* supposed to be?" he demanded, looking Jack up and down.

"Sir?" Jack asked between stiff lips.

"Is this some kind of joke?" Grisko bit out, waving a hand at him.

Jack looked down at Draycos, back in his proper place wrapped around his body. "It's a tattoo, sir."

"It's a tattoo, sir," Grisko mimicked. "Get rid of it."

Jack blinked. "Sir?"

"I said get rid of it," Grisko snapped. "Wash it off, sandblast it off—whatever it takes."

"But it's a tattoo," Jack protested. "It doesn't come off."

Grisko had been starting to turn back toward the door. Instead, he turned back to Jack, gazing down his nose directly into Jack's face. "Are you arguing with me, Montana?" he asked, his voice suddenly very quiet. "Are you disobeying a direct order?"

"No, sir," Jack said, thinking fast. "Request permission to return home to visit a removal clinic."

The corner of Grisko's mouth twitched into something that was probably as close to a smile as he ever got. "That's better," he said. "When I give you an order, you jump to obey it. Clear?"

"Yes, sir," Jack said.

"Good," Grisko said. "Permission denied. You don't skip out on basic for anything. You'll get it removed during first liberty."

He made a precise about-face, just like the ones Jack and the others had practiced the previous afternoon, except that Grisko got it right. "All right, maggots," he announced, starting back down the line. "You've got five minutes to suit up in fatigues and report to the mess hall. Thirty minutes from right now, you will have eaten and assembled on the Number Three parade ground. Now *move!*"

They spent the morning practicing more drills and formations. By the time the lunch trumpet sounded some of them were nearly as good at turns and about-faces as Grisko.

Not that Grisko would ever admit that, of course. To hear him talk and complain, they would never be anything more than undisciplined, incompetent maggots.

Though as Jack watched some of his fellow recruits fumbling around, he had to admit the sergeant might have a point.

After lunch it was more drills, this time with their candy-cane weapons. The extra weight didn't seem that important at first, but after the first hour of spinning it back and forth the Gompers flash rifle in particular began to feel like it was made of solid lead. By midafternoon, whatever crispness had been in their movements was long gone. An hour after that, a couple of the younger kids were whimpering under their breath with the effort.

That was a mistake. Sergeant Grisko disliked whimpering

even more than he disliked full-body dragon tattoos. Each time he caught even a hint of it, he stopped the drill flat and laid into the offender.

One of them was Rogan Mbusu, the eleven-year-old masquerading as fourteen who had so admired Jack's dragon back at the recruitment center. By the time Grisko finished with him and stalked away, Rogan was nearly in tears.

There were, however, two notable exceptions to the group's overall fatigue and clumsiness. One of them was Jommy Randolph, the boy who had complained to Jack about his indenture at the recruitment center. For all his dread back then, he seemed to be quickly settling into the role of the perfect trainee.

Maybe he was good at this. Or maybe he was simply fighting hard to keep from getting shown up.

Because the other exception was Alison Kayna.

Jack found himself watching her as they went through the drills. She was two rows up from Jack's position in the formation and a little to the right, easy enough for him to see without turning his head. Like Jommy, she was quick to pick up the techniques and routines. Unlike Jommy, she didn't seem to be working all that hard at it.

Uncle Virgil had often said that there were only two types of people who could pick up a skill at the drop of a hat. One group was people who already had some idea what they were doing, while the other was natural con artists with an inborn knack for learning new skills. Natural con artists like Jack himself.

Of course, Uncle Virgil had only brought that up when

trying to talk Jack into an especially tricky job. But the point was still valid. Either Alison had already had some military training, or else she was one of those very special people. The first possibility seemed ridiculous. She was only fourteen, after all, hardly ex-StarForce material. But the second wasn't any better. If she was that special, what was she doing in the middle of a small-time mercenary training camp?

The more Jack thought about it, and the more he watched her, the more it bothered him. But there was nothing specific about her behavior that he could put his finger on. He thought about discussing it with Draycos, but aside from the few minutes between lights-out and Draycos taking off for the evening's observation duty there wasn't much time for them to talk.

So he kept his thoughts to himself, and waited for a chance to talk to Alison directly. After all, he was a pretty good thief and con artist, too. With a little luck, he should be able to figure out what she was up to.

To his surprise, it wasn't that easy.

It should have been. It really should have. After all, he and Alison were two of a couple hundred teenagers who'd been thrown into the close quarters of basic training. They were living this soldier stuff; living it, breathing it, dreaming it, and if you globbed enough ketchup on it you could choke it down in the mess hall. It should have been simple to find a way to bump into her during a free moment and strike up a conversation.

There was certainly no lack of possible topics. Sergeant Grisko alone took top three places on any likely list.

But as that first full day turned into the second, and then dragged into the third, Jack discovered the recruits were being allowed very few free moments.

Most of their time was taken up by organized group activities like calisthenics or marching and field drills. At those times he could see Alison, but there was no chance of talking to her. Most of the rest of their day was spent reading from their manuals or sitting in classrooms quoting sections of those manuals back to their instructors.

Mealtimes, which were about as close to free time as they got, were also no good. There weren't a lot of girls in the group to begin with, and they all seemed to cluster together at the same three tables at every meal. Alison, naturally, sat at the center table, which meant Jack would have to push his way through everyone else to get to her.

Which pretty much left the middle of the night. With the barracks blacked out and roving patrols moving around the camp, that was a dead end, too. Even if he had been willing to try, he desperately needed the sleep.

By the fourth day he was half inclined to just give it up. Every muscle ached from the calisthenics, his head hurt from all the technical information he was cramming into it, and he was starting to do parade-ground drills in his dreams. If Alison was pulling some scam on this bunch, he was about ready to sit back and cheer her on.

On the other hand, his own goal here wasn't simply to

survive basic training, either. He couldn't afford to trip over some scheme of Alison's while he was trying to break into the Edge's computer records. One way or another, he had to find out what she was up to.

And so he waited, and watched, and tried to be patient. And on the fifth day, that patience was finally rewarded.

"The targets are set up over there," Sergeant Grisko told them, pointing as the trainees filed by the weapons table that had been set up in the woods. Through the trees, a hundred yards away, Jack could see a ragged edge of rocks. "Go pick a firing position and have at it."

The trainees fanned out through the trees. Gingerly hefting his Gompers flash rifle, Jack headed off toward the right flank. "This is a different style of weapon than the one carried by the Brummga we saw aboard the *Havenseeker*," Draycos murmured from beneath his shirt.

"That one was some kind of machine gun," Jack told him. "It fired bullets. Little projectiles, driven by small explosions."

"I understand the concept."

"Okay. This thing is a chemically pumped laser. Big difference. Hurts just as bad if it goes off in your face, though."

Draycos stirred against his skin. "You seem uncomfortable with it."

"Try scared to death," Jack growled back. "Two hours' worth of training, and we're supposed to know how to fire these things?"

"You are not familiar with this weapon?"

Jack snorted. "You kidding? I don't even like looking at it."

"Yet you were carrying a hand weapon when we first met."

"I was carrying a tangler," Jack corrected tartly. "There's about fifty light-years' difference between that and one of these."

"You!" Grisko called from behind him. "Dragonback!"

Confused, Jack swiveled around. "Sir?"

The sergeant was standing back by the weapons table, his fists resting on his hips. "Someday, if you're really, really good at this, maybe they'll issue you a weapon with a vocal rangefinder chip," Grisko told him. "Until then, don't talk to your gun. It won't talk back."

Jack felt his ears reddening. "Yes, sir," he said. Turning around again, he stalked off through the trees. "Thanks, Draycos," he muttered under his breath. "Like I needed more trouble."

"My apologies," the dragon said quietly.

Jack sighed. "Forget it."

He got a few more steps before Draycos spoke again. "I am still confused."

"A tangler is a nonlethal weapon," Jack explained tiredly. Draycos could go off on bunny trails of his own all day, but once he got an idea or question stuck between those pointy ears, you couldn't shake it loose with a pry bar. "That means it doesn't kill anyone. Hey, you used the thing—you saw what it did."

"I understand the difference," Draycos said, a little stiffly. "I *am* a K'da warrior. My surprise is that someone from your former profession would not be familiar with many different styles of weapons."

Jack shook his head. "You've got it backwards," he said. "Someone in my former profession couldn't afford *not* to be choosy about his choice of guns. Ever hear of felony murder?"

"No."

"A felony is a major crime," Jack explained. A few trees ahead, he could see a section of jagged rocks. It looked like as good a place as any for target practice. "Like armed robbery or kidnapping or something."

"Or murder," Draycos added quietly.

Jack shivered. He'd already seen what Draycos and his K'da warrior ethic thought about murderers. "Anyway, felony murder is when someone dies while you're committing a crime like that."

"Even if you did not intend for it to happen?"

"Even if it wasn't even your fault," Jack said. "No matter how it happens, if you were the one committing the crime, you can be charged with murder. That's why Uncle Virgil and I never, ever carried weapons that could kill."

"Interesting," Draycos said thoughtfully. "K'da and Shontine law requires intent to be considered. Is this universal in the Orion Arm?"

"On most Internos planets it is," Jack told him. "A lot of the alien worlds do things differently."

"Stop," Draycos said suddenly.

Jack froze, half concealed behind a particularly large tree. "What?" he demanded, his eyes flicking around.

"Beyond this tree is open ground," Draycos said. "You must go low to cross it."

"Oh, for—" Jack threw a glare down at his shirt. "It *is* only a training exercise, you know."

"Then let us properly train you," Draycos said. "Go low."

Jack sighed. "Just what I've always wanted," he muttered, slinging the Gompers over his back and getting down on his hands and knees. "My own personal drill sergeant."

"Use your center joints," Draycos advised. "You will stay lower and be able to move more quickly."

"My center—? Oh. Knees and elbows."

"Correct. I am surprised they have not already taught you that."

Jack frowned as he started across the patch of open ground toward the rocks ahead. Come to think of it, why hadn't they?

The knees-elbows waddle was easier than he would have expected. It was still a lot more awkward than just walking, though. Reaching a convenient notch in the rocks, he carefully eased his head up for a look.

He was at the edge of a large gravel pit that stretched out for probably a hundred yards, maybe fifty feet deep at its lowest point. A dozen electronic targets had been set up at various places in the pit.

"Nothing like starting us off at long-range work," Jack muttered, unlimbering his rifle and flipping off the safety. "Whatever happened to 'Don't fire until you see the whites of their eyes'?"

"Pardon?"

"Skip it." At least there was a conveniently shaped notch on top of one of the rocks where he could brace the rifle. Setting the muzzle into the notch, he started to get to his knees.

"Keep your head down," a girl's voice ordered.

Frowning, Jack rolled over onto his side and looked behind him.

It was Alison Kayna.

CHAPTER 6

She was coming from the trees behind him, wriggling across the open ground using the same elbows-and-knees crawl Draycos had just taught him. Naturally, she was doing it better. "What did you say?" he asked.

"I said keep your head down," she repeated, angling toward a section of rock near Jack's. "They'll have snipers targeting us from the far side of the gravel pit."

Jack shrunk down a little behind the protection of the rocks. "Snipers?"

"You don't think this is just target practice, do you?" Alison asked, puffing a little as she reached the rocks. "You've seen the games Grisko likes to play. You think he'd pass up a golden opportunity like this?"

"A golden opportunity for what?" Jack demanded. Suddenly the rock he was leaning against didn't feel nearly so solid and secure anymore. "Blowing our heads off?"

"Oh, get real," she scolded, unslinging her Gompers from across her back. "They'll just be using marker lasers."

"Never heard of them."

"They cause a mild skin reaction. You don't even feel it, but the mark shows up like a spot of sunburn."

Jack began to breathe a little easier. "Temporary, I hope."

"It lasts a day or two." Alison eased an eye up into a gap between two rocks. "Shows where you got careless."

"Nice of them to tell us about this," Jack grumbled, rolling back onto his stomach and sidling his way over toward a lower and better protected gap in the rocks. "Good thing you know your way around this stuff."

"I did some research," Alison said. "I gather you didn't."

"Not really," Jack said. He lined up his sights on one of the distant targets, wondering if someone across the way was lining up sights on him. "I figured they'd be giving us all the training we needed."

"I wasn't talking about training," Alison said. "But that's another point."

Carefully, Jack squeezed the trigger. There was a brief flash of laser light accompanied by a soft hiss, and the spent power cartridge ejected from the chamber. It rolled across the grass, trailing the stink of chemical reactant behind it. "What's another point?"

"The training." There was a hiss from her direction as she squeezed off a shot of her own. "Doesn't it strike you as odd that we haven't even gotten to look at real weapons until now?"

Jack shrugged, lining up on another target. "It's only been five days," he pointed out.

"Out of a total of ten," she countered. "Ten days of basic training, then off we go. With most armies, this would run six weeks or more."

"Yeah, but most of them would be going off to real wars," Jack reminded her. "We'll just be doing garrison support duty."

"That's what Grisko *says*," she said ominously. There were two more hisses from her position. "You run into a boy named Rogan Mbusu yet?"

"Sure," Jack said. "Short kid, big ears. Claims to be fourteen."

Alison snorted. "Yeah, I've talked to him," she said scornfully. "He's lucky if he's even seen twelve. Legally, you know, you're only supposed to indenture kids fourteen and older."

"So the Edge bends the rules a little," Jack said. "What's your point?"

"My point is I don't want to do even garrison duty with some kid who's too young to know which end of his rifle goes where," she said darkly. "Garrison workers can get just as dead as regular troops, you know."

Jack grimaced. "You sound like my uncle. How come you know so much?"

"Like I said, research," she said.

"Like my Aunt Fanny," Jack retorted. "Come on, you didn't get this from any book."

Her lips compressed into a thin line. "If you must know, this is my second try at this," she said. "I washed out of the first merc group I was indentured to."

"And you came back for more?"

She shot him an icy glare. "My parents need the money.

Yours don't?" Without waiting for a reply, she turned back to her shooting.

Which was just as well, since Jack didn't have a ready answer for that one.

For a few minutes they shot side by side in silence. Jack alternated between several targets, wondering how he was doing. Probably pretty lousy. Grisko would have a way of matching up the hits to each of the trainees' guns after they were all done, but that didn't do Jack any good right now.

"Why 'Dragonback'?" Alison asked suddenly.

Jack frowned. "What?"

"Grisko called you Dragonback earlier. When you walked off talking to your gun."

Jack's ears reddened again. Probably the whole group had heard that. Terrific. "I have a tattoo of a dragon across my back," he said. "A big one."

"Something to do with the old Dragonback warriors?"

"Nope," Jack assured her. "In fact, I never even heard of them until a month ago."

She grunted and resumed her firing. Five minutes later, her clip of cartridges was empty. "I'm off," she announced, slinging the Gompers over her back again and starting backwards in a reverse elbows-and-knees crawl. "Make sure you fire your whole clip before going back if you don't want Grisko to scorch your ears off. Hitting the targets once in awhile would be nice, too."

"Thanks," Jack said dryly. "I'll see what I can do."

"And keep your head down," she warned.

A minute later, she was gone, vanished into the cover of the trees. "Well, that was fun," he muttered.

"She has great courage," Draycos said. "I can hear it in her voice."

"Or else she's just plain stupid," Jack said, picking a target and firing off a round at it. "Her and her family both. How do people let themselves get so desperate for money?"

"Many times it is not their fault."

"Most of the time it is," Jack said stubbornly.

"That sounds like your Uncle Virgil's philosophy."

"Leave Uncle Virgil out of this," Jack said, firing two more shots. Missing both, probably. "Anyway, he knew how the real world worked."

There was a short silence, just long enough for Jack to realize that Draycos could easily have reminded him what Uncle Virgil had done for a living. "Have you no compassion for the weak?" the dragon asked instead.

"Compassion wasn't a big priority where I grew up," Jack said. "And I never saw it do anyone any good."

"No one?"

Jack glanced a glare down at him. "How come we only have these big moral discussions when Uncle Virge isn't around to help me defend myself?"

"Do such discussions make you uncomfortable?"

Jack shook his head impatiently. "Can we just skip this?"

"Of course," Draycos said, as if he hadn't been the one who'd brought it up in the first place. "Shall I give you my report on the nighttime patrols?"

"Yeah, sure," Jack said. "Go ahead."

"There are four separate teams," Draycos said. "Two soldiers in each. They pass within view of the main headquarters' entrance approximately once every twenty minutes."

"How regular is that twenty minutes?" Jack asked.

"Close, but not exact," Draycos said. "The period has ranged from eighteen to twenty-five minutes."

"Do they always come from the same directions each time?"

"Again, approximately," the dragon said. "I have noted slight differences in the direction of approach, but nothing significant."

"A regular patrol pattern, then," Jack decided, his annoyance at the dragon forgotten. Draycos might be the local expert on morals and ethics, but putting puzzle pieces together was where Jack got to shine. "If there's one thing Uncle Virgil taught me to love, it's regular patterns."

"There may still be alarms on the doors," Draycos warned.

"I'm sure there are," Jack agreed. "And on the computer, too. But I know how to handle those. My biggest worry was getting shot on the way there."

"Do we then make our attempt tonight?"

Jack fired his last two rounds while he considered. "Let's give it one more night," he said. "If the patrol pattern is still the same, we'll go tomorrow."

"And if we are successful?"

"Well, we're sure not going to hang around any longer than we have to," Jack told him, slinging his rifle and starting to back up. As before, the technique felt a lot more awkward than Alison had made it look. "If Uncle Virge is on the ball, he'll have the *Essenay* stashed somewhere nearby. Once we've pulled everything the Edge has on Djinn-90 fighters, we'll whistle him up and get out of here."

"And if we do not find what we need?"

"If they've got it, we'll find it," Jack said confidently. "If not . . . well, we'll worry about that when it happens."

He reached the cover of the trees and stood up. "Come on. Let's go see how I did."

"Not very well, I am afraid," Draycos said. "But do not be discouraged. Long-range shooting is difficult to master."

"It could have been a lot harder," Jack pointed out. "A machine gun, or even a semiautomatic projectile rifle . . ." He trailed off, a strange thought striking him.

"Is there trouble?" Draycos asked.

"I was just thinking," Jack said slowly. "A flash rifle doesn't have any kick. No recoil. You understand?"

"Yes."

"That makes it a lot easier to learn," Jack went on. "But it's also a whole lot more expensive to shoot. Does that sound like the kind of weapon you'd want beginners to start with?"

Draycos was silent a moment. "You are being taught to march and stand in formation," he said. "From your books you are being taught the words and expressions soldiers use, and a great deal of technical information. Now you are learning how to shoot the easiest of possible weapons."

"*And,* if you believe Alison's numbers, all of this is happening in a quarter of the time regular soldiers need for their training," Jack finished for him. "This is starting to feel a little creepy."

"Yet as you yourself said, you are only being trained as garrison assistants," Draycos reminded him. "Perhaps this is adequate for such duty."

"Maybe," Jack said. "But like Alison said, you can get just as dead in a garrison as you can out in the field."

Still, he reminded himself as he continued through the trees, he wouldn't be staying for that part of the operation. Tomorrow night he and Draycos would pull the information they needed, and then they would be out of here. "Anyway, I'll bet I did better than you think," he added.

"You have a tendency to shoot high," Draycos told him.

"I do not," Jack insisted. "You wait and see. You'll be eating those words for your dinner."

"Pardon?"

Jack sighed. "Skip it."

Alison and Jommy, to Jack's complete lack of surprise, came out first and second in the final tally.

To his rather annoyed surprise, he found that Draycos's evaluation of his own shooting skills had been correct. He himself had finished a less than glorious eighty-seventh.

But at least he'd only collected three sniper hits. Most of the others, blissfully unaware of their true position in Grisko's shooting gallery, had up to two dozen of the little marks.

Alison, naturally, had only one.

Dinner that night was grumpier than usual. Most of the recruits seemed to think it had been a highly unfair trick to play on them, and the majority seemed to blame Sergeant Grisko personally for it. Jommy in particular was highly indignant, apparently feeling that his twenty-one hits took a lot away from his otherwise impressive second-place score.

Jack stayed out of the debate as best he could. There was no need to get them thinking about his own low sniper hit rate. It might lead to the unpleasant suspicion that he had been in on the scam from the start.

After dinner there was a twilight marching drill, using real Gompers flash rifles this time instead of the candy canes. Unloaded, fortunately. Then came more study time, bedtime preparations, and finally lights-out. Jack waited until the rest of the barracks was asleep, then gave Draycos his meager meal and sent him to his washroom window to watch.

It was somewhere in the middle of the night when he suddenly awoke.

For a minute he lay motionless in bed, trying to figure out what had awakened him. Then, suddenly, he got it.

There was a rush of cool air rippling over him from the washroom area where Draycos was supposed to be watching. Not the usual light breeze that came from having the window open a crack while the dragon peered out, but something stronger.

Silently, he climbed out of bed and padded barefoot across the cold floor to the washroom. If this was nothing but a matter of the wind having shifted direction during the night, he promised himself darkly, he was going to be very annoyed.

The wind hadn't shifted direction. The breeze was stronger because the window had been propped wide open.

And Draycos was gone.

CHAPTER 7

All right, Jack told himself urgently. *Don't panic.* Draycos wasn't lost, after all. He was just misplaced a little.

All right. First off, it was for sure that none of the roving patrols could have gotten him. Certainly not without making a *lot* of noise in the process. Wherever Draycos had gotten to, he'd gotten there voluntarily.

Could he have decided to tackle the HQ building on his own? Ridiculous. Draycos might be a first-class warrior, but he didn't know the first thing about human-designed locks and alarms. He wouldn't have gone there without Jack.

And then the obvious answer struck him. Of course: Draycos was hungry. After nearly a week of the starvation diet Jack had put him on, the dragon had finally given up and gone hunting.

Jack felt his face warm with shame. He should have tried better to bring Draycos more food. Tried, nothing—he should have *done* better. But with all those kids bustling around, and Grisko and the other drill instructors likely to drop in without warning—

He shook his head firmly. Those were cheap excuses. And as Uncle Virgil would have said, yesterday's cheap excuses were tomorrow's fish wrap. As of tomorrow, he would starting bringing a decent meal home to his partner.

Partner. He frowned at the word. Uncle Virge didn't want him to have any partners. Uncle Virge especially didn't want him having a partner with Draycos's rigid, self-sacrificing K'da warrior ethic. Uncle Virge would be very unhappy if he knew Jack was starting to think of Draycos in that way.

The open window was next to the low wall of the wash-room's big shower area. Carefully, trying not to make any noise, Jack pulled himself up onto the wall. He steadied himself with a grip on the edge of the window and looked out.

The camp was actually rather pretty by starlight. To look on it now you wouldn't think there was so much grunting and sweating and agony out there during the day. He looked through the trees toward the dark windows of the headquarters building, trying to imagine what kind of security they might have there.

And then, he caught a flicker of movement from his right. Something that looked like a black shadow was moving swiftly and silently along the ground toward the barracks.

It was Draycos. It had to be. And the fact that the dragon's golden scales had turned to combat black meant there was trouble.

He slid off the wall onto the shower area's tile floor. If Draycos was moving that fast down there, he wasn't likely to slow down much coming through the window.

He didn't. Without any hint of warning, the dragon was suddenly there, leaping with bull's-eye accuracy straight through the center of the opening. His tail caught the edge of the window with a soft slap as he passed, slowing him down and deflecting his arc just enough to drop him soundlessly into the center of the shower area.

"What's the matter?" Jack hissed.

Draycos did a startled spin, twisting around like a cat on a hot charcoal grill. The sudden arching of his neck crest relaxed as he saw it was Jack. "I went out to better study the movements of the patrols," the dragon said, his tail twitching restlessly. "I am sorry, but I may have been seen."

Jack glanced up at the window. "Where?"

"To the north," Draycos said. "I heard movement nearby and went up into the trees."

"What happened then?"

"I eluded the patrols without difficulty," Draycos said. "I do not think they really know what they are looking for. But they may still be searching for me. I am sorry."

"Wait a second," Jack said as a sudden thought struck him. "The patrols are off chasing each other's tails up north?"

"They have gone all directions," Draycos said. "From the movements of lights, it would seem they are searching the entire perimeter of the camp."

"Are they, now," Jack said, scratching his cheek. "All of them, you think?"

The tail twitching suddenly stopped. "What are you suggesting?" Draycos asked cautiously.

Jack nodded toward the window. "I'm thinking this might be a good time to go crash the party."

Draycos's neck crest stiffened a little. "But the patrols are on alert."

"Right," Jack agreed. "But they're on alert somewhere else. Give me a second to get dressed."

Two minutes later he was back. Draycos had closed the window down to a crack again and was crouched on top of the shower wall peering out. With the immediate excitement over, his scales had returned to their usual red-edged gold. "I see and hear no evidence of movement," he reported. "But I am not convinced this is a wise move."

"The worst that can happen is that we have to dodge the patrols," Jack pointed out as he pulled on the thin plastic camouflage gloves that had come with his field kit. No point leaving fingerprints or traces of sweat where someone could find them. "If we wait until tomorrow, we'll have to do that anyway. At least here we start with an open playing field."

"Tomorrow the patrols will be on a known schedule," Draycos countered. But nevertheless he pushed open the window and slid through.

Climbing up onto the shower wall, Jack got his legs through the opening and followed. The window was pretty high, and as he lowered himself he wondered briefly about his chances of twisting an ankle as he hit the ground.

He needn't have worried. Draycos had taken up position beneath the window, stretching up on his hind legs with his front paws braced against the wall. Jack's feet found spots on the dragon's shoulders, and a second later he was safely on the ground.

"Looks clear," Jack whispered as they crouched together beside the barracks. "Let's go."

Draycos put a paw on Jack's outstretched hand and disappeared up the sleeve. Jack waited until he had slithered along his skin to his usual position with his head at Jack's right shoulder. Then, with one final look around, he headed off toward the headquarters building at a quick trot.

He had paced off the distance two days ago on his way to the mess hall and knew it to be about a hundred yards. Sneaking through the trees in the dead of night, senses alert for trouble, it seemed a lot farther.

There were no shouts of discovery as they reached the front corner of the headquarters building. "Do we enter through the main door?" Draycos murmured.

"Probably not," Jack puffed. "But I'll check."

One glance was all it took. "Not a chance," he told the dragon, slipping around the side of the building. "The lock's armed six ways from August. We're not going to pop it without a set of tools."

"What then?" Draycos asked.

"We find a likely window," Jack said, pausing at the first window and giving its edge a quick examination. "Maybe on the second floor where they might not be so careful."

"Or perhaps the third?" Draycos's head lifted out of Jack's shoulder, pushing aside the shirt material. His tongue flicked out, pointing toward the stars.

Jack looked up. Directly above them, two windows up, was a darkened third floor window. Even in the dim light, he could see it was open a few inches. "Looks promising," he agreed doubtfully. "Can you jump that high?"

"Brace yourself," Draycos said in reply. "What do I do when I am inside?"

"Find a way down here," Jack told him, pointing at the first-floor window in front of them. "Doesn't look like there's too much of an alarm here. I should be able to talk you through the disarming procedure."

"Very well. Are you ready?"

Jack planted his feet firmly against the ground and loosened his shirt at the back. "Ready."

An instant later he was nearly knocked off his feet as the dragon leaped upward from his back, his front paws shoving down hard on Jack's shoulders for momentum as they passed. Before Jack could even flail for balance the dragon's rear paws thudded down in the same spots, giving himself an extra push upward. Jack grabbed for the edge of the window in front of him, nearly putting his hand through the plastic in the process, and looked up.

Draycos was hanging by his front paws from the third-floor window ledge. For a moment he peered inside, his tongue flicking through the gap to taste the air. Then, working his snout into the opening, he pushed upward, levering the window all the way open. A quick pull, a lunge of golden scales, and he was inside.

Jack turned and looked at the silent woods and the darkened buildings half-seen through them. With Draycos gone, he suddenly felt a lot more exposed out here. He hoped the dragon would hurry.

Too late, he also hoped the Edge hadn't loaded their headquarters with hidden security cameras. Getting Draycos recorded on videotube would be all they needed.

The light touch that brushed across his shoulder was like

a high-voltage electric shock. He twitched violently, nearly wrenching his back as he twisted around, half expecting to see Sergeant Grisko grinning at him over the muzzle of a gun.

It wasn't Grisko. It wasn't a gun, either. It was, instead, the plug end of an electrical extension cord.

He looked up. Draycos had reappeared in the window, the cord dangling from between his front paws. "A change of plan," he whispered down at Jack. "It may be safer to stay on this floor."

Jack took a deep breath, sternly ordering his heart to start beating again. "Right," he muttered. Getting a grip on the cord, he started to climb.

Between his climbing and Draycos's pulling, he made it up and through the window in record time. "It appears to be an assembly area," the dragon suggested as Jack peered around at the long tables stacked with electronics gear.

"Probably maintenance," Jack said, his nose wrinkling at the faint stench of burned insulation. The smell was probably why whoever worked here had decided to leave the window open overnight. "I don't see any computers, though," he added, closing the window back down to its original crack.

The dragon's ears twitched toward the closed door. "I hear no movement outside."

"Good," Jack said, heading toward the door. A gray plastic bag caught his eye as he passed, and he scooped it up. "Hold it a second," he added as Draycos reached for the door handle. "They may have cameras out there."

He slid his hands into the bag, stretching the heavy plastic taut. "Here—you've got the claws in the family," he said. "Cut me a couple of eye holes, will you?"

Draycos's neck arched and he extended a claw. A couple of quick slashes, and he had a neat slit visor carved into the plastic. "Will that do?"

"Let's see," Jack said, wincing a little as he slid the bag over his head. He'd seen those claws slice grooves in solid metal, and they'd come a little too close to his hands just now.

The positioning was perfect. The bag settled onto the top of his head with the slit directly in front of his eyes. And unlike the eye holes he'd asked for, the slit even allowed him some peripheral vision. "Perfect," he told the dragon. "Get aboard and let's go."

The hallway outside was dark and silent. Jack stayed close to the wall, trying to ignore the rustling of the plastic bag in his ears. The main offices would probably be on the first and second floors, but with luck one of the rooms up here would have the computer link he needed.

He struck gold with the second room he tried. Not only were there three terminals in the center of the room, but two of the walls were lined with file cabinets.

"Bingo," Jack murmured as he closed the door behind him. "Looks like we've found the main file room."

Draycos's head rose from Jack's shoulder, his green eyes glittering in the dim starlight filtering in through the window. "We have found old records," he corrected. "The labels on the cabinets indicate the information is over five years old."

Jack felt his lip twist. So much for hunting down the right tube and studying it later in the safety and convenience of the barracks. "Well, we can't expect them to just hand it to us," he said philosophically, closing the door and heading for the computers. "You want to keep watch?"

Draycos dropped to the floor from his sleeve. He opened the door a crack and pressed his ear to the opening. "Do not take too long," he warned.

"Thanks," Jack said dryly, turning on the computer. "I wouldn't have thought of that."

"Will there not be code-locks?" the dragon asked, ignoring the sarcasm.

"Like cold on ice."

"Pardon?"

"They'll be all over the place," Jack translated. "But Uncle Virgil taught me a few tricks."

For a few minutes he worked in silence. The sewer-rat approach, as Uncle Virgil had called this technique, was nearly always effective with human-designed computers.

Trouble was, it was also pretty slow. Jack could feel sweat gathering on his forehead beneath his mask as he punched the keys. Sooner or later, he knew, the patrols out there were going to get tired of their search and come home. The computer chugged on, the sewer-rat code words chewing away at the defenses.

And then, abruptly, Draycos stiffened. "Footsteps," he hissed. "Someone is coming."

CHAPTER 8

For a second Jack hesitated. To give up now, when they were so close . . . "Where?" he hissed back.

"On the stairway at the near end of the corridor," Draycos said. "Moving slowly upward."

"Which floor?" Jack asked. "I mean, are they coming from first to second or second to third?"

Draycos's other ear twitched toward the cracked door. "First to second," he said. "And there is only one person."

Jack chewed at his lip. A single person implied a night watchman making his rounds. If he went through the second floor before coming up here to the third, there might still be time to find and pull the records he needed.

And then Draycos's tongue flicked out. "There is an odd odor," he said. "It tastes . . . unpleasant."

Frowning, Jack crossed to his side. "Let me smell," he whispered. The dragon moved away, and Jack took a careful sniff.

One was enough. "We're out of here," he muttered, closing the door all the way and heading for the window at the far side of the room. As he passed the computer, he shut it off. "Come on."

"What is it?" Draycos asked, hurrying to catch up with him.

"He's laying a sopor mist ahead of himself," Jack said, looking around. Unfortunately, this room hadn't come equipped with any handy extension cords. "A few more whiffs and you and I would have been snoozing blissfully away. You see anything to climb with?"

"No need," Draycos said, stepping to the window. With forepaws and muzzle he slid it open. "I will jump first and stand below. You may drop onto my back."

"You must be kidding," Jack growled, going back to the desks. The computers themselves were standard fold-top portables, with a whole spaghetti mix of cables connecting them to printers and scanners and other equipment. "I'd break your back. Or else miss completely and break mine. Help me get these cables loose."

Two minutes later, Jack had the cables knotted together. "It will be too short," Draycos warned, running an eye over the makeshift rope.

"It'll be close enough," Jack insisted, carrying the lumpy coil across the room and feeding one end out the window. "Here," he added, handing the other end to the dragon. "Hold tight."

There was no way he could slide down quickly, not on a rope with as many knots in it as this one had. Just the same, he went down as fast as he could manage. The watchman back there could burst in on Draycos at any time, and he probably had something a lot nastier than sopor mist in his arsenal.

But there were no shots from above, and none of the knots gave way, and a few seconds later he had reached the end. Draycos had been right; he found his feet dangling about six feet short of the ground. Bending his knees slightly, he dropped the rest of the way.

He'd barely landed when the collection of cables fell into a heap beside him. Draycos was right behind them, dropping into a crouch away from the tangle. "Anyone nearby?" Jack whispered.

The dragon's long neck turned back and forth, his green eyes glowing like a pair of control panel status lights as they probed the darkness. His tongue darted out, and his ears twitched back and forth like small, pointed radar dishes. "I sense no one," he said.

"Okay." Pulling off his bag mask, Jack tossed it to the breeze. It would have been nice to have its protection all the way back to the barracks, but he didn't dare risk it getting caught in some bush nearby once he finally threw it away. Grisko and his buddies would come hunting for the intruder soon enough, and marking which of the three barracks he had come from would be making it far too easy for them. He would just have to trust that Draycos was right about the coast being clear. "Let's go."

The trip seemed even longer this direction than it had going the other way. But again, there were no shouts or lights or other signs of discovery. Either they'd made it out ahead of the general alarm, or else Grisko had decided to play it cool. Draycos boosted Jack up to the window, then followed.

Three minutes later, undressed again, he was safely back under the blankets.

"What now?" the dragon murmured from his shoulder.

Jack took a slow, deep breath, listening to his heart thudding in his ears. That had been close. Too close. Uncle Virge would definitely not be happy with this one.

Especially since they hadn't even accomplished what they'd set out to do. "I don't know," he had to admit. "If we hadn't left that pile of computer cables on the ground, they might have figured it was a false alarm. No chance of that now, though."

"My fault," Draycos said, his whisper sounding subdued. "I am accustomed to thinking as a warrior. Not as—" He paused.

"A thief?" Jack suggested.

"Yes," Draycos said reluctantly. "I apologize. I know you are trying to move away from that part of your life."

"It's okay," Jack soothed him. "Actually, it's kind of nice to know I've got something useful to bring to this team."

"You are the reason I am alive," Draycos reminded him. "For my part, that is very useful."

"And you're very welcome for it," Jack said. "I just meant it's good to be something other than your personal RV."

"Pardon?"

"Recreational vehicle. Mobile home." Jack shook his head. "Skip it."

"Ah. I see."

"Anyway, don't worry about the cables," Jack went on. "Even if you'd thought to pull them back inside, leaving them tied together like that would still have been a dead give-away. You sure didn't have time to put everything back the way it was."

"What will we do next?"

Jack stared at the dark underside of the bunk above him. "Depends on whether they nail us or not," he said. "If they grab me tomorrow, we wait our chance and try to break out."

"It would be useful in that case to have transport ready."

Jack peered down his nose at his chest. "Are you suggesting we ask Uncle Virge for help? *You?*"

"My feelings about Uncle Virge's life philosophy do not prevent me from working with him," Draycos said stiffly. He shifted a little across Jack's skin, like a K'da version of fidgeting.

"Even if Uncle Virge isn't exactly your sort of soul mate?"

"I do not know that word," the dragon growled. "The point remains. I am a poet-warrior of the K'da. My personal feelings cannot be permitted to intrude upon my work."

"Glad to hear it," Jack said, rather enjoying this. Draycos was always so calm and in control that it was nice to see him squirm a little for a change. "I'll make sure I have my comm clip along tomorrow in case we have to whistle him up."

"Assuming he is close enough to be of assistance."

"He is," Jack assured him. "Anyway, if they *don't* grab me, we might as well finish the last four days of training before we take off."

"We will not try again?"

"With them alerted?" Jack retorted. "Not a chance. We'll have to pick another mercenary group and try again."

"Then why not leave now?"

"Because it'll be easier to sneak out after graduation than before," Jack told him. "And because Alison has proved it helps if you're not starting from scratch."

"Perhaps," Draycos said, sounding doubtful. "We must be alert, though. They may decide not to take you immediately."

"Oh, I'll be careful," Jack said. "Trust me. I've had enough people do that slow vulture circle around me, watching and hoping I'll make a wrong move. I know what it looks like."

"That will be helpful," Draycos said, not sounding entirely convinced. "You had best sleep now."

"Sounds good to me," Jack said with a sigh. The excitement and tension of their midnight excursion was fading, and his eyelids were suddenly feeling very heavy. "See you at reveille."

"Yes," Draycos murmured. "I wonder . . ."

With an effort, Jack propped open one eyelid. "You wonder what?"

"I wonder if perhaps I was not seen at all," the dragon said. "Perhaps it was something else that drew the patrols to the camp perimeter."

"Such as?"

"Perhaps the *Essenay*," Draycos said. "You suggested it would be close at hand."

Jack thought it over. It *was* possible, he had to admit. After five days of not hearing from him, Uncle Virge might well have gotten impatient and brought the ship in for a closer look. Without knowing the Edge's security system, he could have tripped some alarm in the process. "Could be," he told

Draycos. "We'll ask him about it later." He lifted his eyebrows. "If it *was* Uncle Virge, you have my permission to never let him live it down."

"I was not thinking of how to place blame," the dragon said. "I was merely wondering if the ship might have taken damage."

Jack winced. "I guess we'll find that out soon enough, too."

CHAPTER 9

No one came storming into the barracks in the predawn darkness before reveille. No one came and grabbed him in the shower, or on his way to breakfast, or even at breakfast. Everything, in fact, settled nicely into the normal morning routine, from the rotten food to the blaring trumpet calling the recruits to the morning parade-ground maneuver.

It wasn't until they'd finished the first two drills that the routine was abruptly broken.

He spotted the officer angling across the field toward Grisko as the sergeant shouted out the commands that ended the second drill. Grisko set the recruits to attention and for a moment he and the officer talked quietly together. Then the officer turned to face the trainees, and Jack saw that it was Lieutenant Basht from the recruiting office.

"All right, listen up," Grisko bellowed across the ranks. "The following fall out and go with Lieutenant Basht: Brinkster, Kayna, Li, Mbusu, Montana, Randolph."

The sodden breakfast, which had already been lying heavily on Jack's stomach, suddenly picked up about a ton of extra weight. Heart pounding in his ears, he left his position and moved up through the ranks.

"Form up: two by three," Basht ordered as the six recruits reached the front. They did so, Alison and Jommy taking the front two spots. Jack stepped into place behind Jommy, with Rogan Mbusu falling in behind him. Brinkster and Li, both girls, took their places behind Alison.

Basht glanced over their formation, and for a second Jack thought he was going to make some snide comment. But he merely did a crisp military turn and strode off the field.

They followed, automatically falling into step with him. As they walked, Jack tried to puzzle out what was going on.

His analysis didn't get very far. Jommy and Alison were certainly the best of the bunch, which might imply this group had been singled out for special commendation. Problem was, he and Rogan were here, too, and neither of them was exactly near the top of the list. As for Brinkster and Li, Jack had noticed them along the way but neither had struck him as being either particularly good or particularly bad. So ordinary and unnoticeable were they, in fact, that he'd never even heard their first names.

Maybe it was a random sample, then. But with a hundred eighty boys and only twenty girls in the group, it didn't seem likely that a spin of the dart board would end up with three of each.

He was still trying to come up with some explanation when he suddenly realized that Lieutenant Basht was leading them straight toward the headquarters building.

Jack's heart had been starting to quiet down. Now, it picked up its pace again. So that was it. They'd figured out somehow that he was last night's casual visitor, and this whole thing was a smokescreen to get him away from the main group.

Beneath his shirt, he felt Draycos shifting around against his skin. Apparently, the K'da had figured it out, too. "Easy," he muttered a warning. The first rule Uncle Virgil had hammered into him when facing the authorities was not to do their job for them. *You're innocent until they absolutely prove otherwise,* he had told Jack over and over. *And for ten minutes after that, too,* he'd usually added.

There didn't seem to be any extra security hanging around the building as Basht opened the door and led the way inside. Jack rather expected him to take them straight upstairs to the records room, or maybe to split Jack off from the others and take him up there. To his mild surprise, Basht led them instead to a first-floor room.

To his even greater surprise, the room was filled with computer stations. The stations were unoccupied, but a thin man wearing colonel's insignia was standing near the front beside a double stack of sealed cartons. From the way he eyed them as they filed in, Jack guessed he'd been waiting specifically for them.

"Parade rest," Basht ordered as they formed into their two-by-three again. "Mbusu. Tell me about Sunright."

Sunright? Frantically, Jack searched his memory. Then he remembered: it was one of the worlds that had been listed in the *Current Whinyard's Edge Missions* section of their training manual.

And that was about all he remembered. If Basht called on him, he was going to be in serious trouble.

For a second it looked like Rogan was already there. "Uh—" the boy floundered. His voice quavered the way it always did whenever he had to talk to a superior officer, and Jack winced in sympathy.

Then the mental wheels seemed to catch. "Sunright, sir," Rogan said, his voice still trembling a little. "Third planet of the Gamma Lartrin system. Human colonized in 2115; ceded to the Parprins and Agri by the Treaty of Mcdougall in—"

"Lose the sniveling," Basht cut him off. "Kayna? What are the Edge's interests in the place?"

"The Edge has been hired by a Parprin daublite mining colony to protect its interests from a group of Agrist claim-jumpers," Alison said briskly. So she was on top of this, too. That figured. "Troops have been in position on the ground for the past sixteen months."

"Planetary bio stats?"

"Atmosphere is slightly oxygen-heavy, but well within human tolerances," Alison said. "Gravity is three percent less than Earth Standard; temperatures average two degrees cooler."

Basht nodded. "Who are we facing there? Randolph?"

"The Agri have their local military group," Jommy said. "Mostly volunteers. They've also hired units of the Shamshir mercenaries."

"Relative strengths?" Basht asked. "Li?"

Li seemed to shrink behind the smooth skin of her face. "I don't remember, sir," she said in a barely audible voice.

For a long second Basht's eyes burned into her, as if he

was trying to set her on fire. Then, the glare flicked over her shoulder. "Brinkster? What's our strength?"

Out of the corner of his eye Jack saw the girl wince. "I think we have eight hundred troops on the ground, sir."

"You *think?*"

"We have eight hundred troops, sir," she said, more firmly this time.

"And the Shamshir?" Basht asked, his eyes finally focusing on Jack. "Montana?"

Jack braced himself to follow Li down in flames. But even as he opened his mouth to tell Basht he didn't know, there were seven rapid pinpricks on the back of his forearm, the urgent tapping of a K'da claw. "They have seven hundred, sir," he said, hoping he was reading Draycos's signal right.

He held his breath. Basht's eyes flicked again to Li, as if silently pointing out that she was the only one not up to speed here. Then he turned and nodded curtly to the colonel. "Sir."

He stepped back as the colonel came forward, and Jack let out a silent sigh of relief. He hadn't realized that during all those hours of study Draycos had actually been reading the manual over his shoulder. Lucky for him.

Over his shoulder. On top of his shoulder. Whatever.

"My name is Colonel Elkor," the other introduced himself. "Late yesterday we received word from Sunright that the Shamshir have made a major blunder. We've been nibbling around the edges of their main InterWorld transmission station, so they've set up a new one. It's in a mountainous area marked as November Six on our maps."

He looked them all over, as if expecting them all to know where November Six was. Jack tried to remember if the Missions section had included a map of the Sunright area, but he couldn't.

"The convenient part about that is that we happen to have a forward observation outpost in that region," Elkor went on. "That means that if we put some specialized computer equipment in there, we'll be able to tap directly into all their off-planet transmissions."

He jerked his head back at the boxes he'd been standing beside when the group came in. "Those are the computers," he said. "You are now the computer operators. Any questions?"

There was a moment of uncertain silence. "Why *aren't* there any questions?" Elkor demanded. "You all already know everything?"

Jommy lifted a hesitant hand. "Sir? I don't know anything about communications work."

"That's better," Elkor rumbled. "Fact is, none of you do. That's why you're here. Lieutenant Basht will be running you through three days of training that will include electronic eavesdropping, decoding, and some preliminary analysis techniques."

"Plus giving you all the access codes you'll need to work our systems," Basht added. "By the time you're done, each of you will be a fully qualified Whinyard's Edge systems operator."

"I presume none of you objects to a change in specialties?" Elkor said, lifting his eyebrows. "If you do, say so now. Plenty of other recruits marching back and forth out there for us to choose from."

The implications were obvious: stay here and do inside work, or go back outside and sweat. There was another silence from the group, this one a lot more positive than the last. "Good," Elkor said briskly. "The six of you are now designated as Technical Squad Tango Five Zulu. Carry on, Lieutenant."

He strode from the room. "All right," Basht said, gesturing toward the computer stations. "Everyone pick a station, and let's get started."

They took a short break for lunch, and an even shorter one for dinner. Throughout the day the noise outside rose and fell as the rest of the recruits were drilled and exercised, then taken away for more target practice, then brought back for more drills and exercise.

The noise inside the room, consisting mostly of Basht's steady drone of information, seemed to go on forever.

The sky was already darkening when they were finally turned loose. "I guess that's what they mean by information overload," Jack commented to Draycos as he trudged alone toward the barracks. "My head is so full it hurts."

"Perhaps the next two days will be easier," Draycos suggested from his shoulder. "You seem to have been given most of the necessary information."

"Yeah, but the next thing will be drilling us in how to use

it," Jack pointed out. "That's always a lot harder than just memorizing facts and figures."

He glanced down at the dragon's head, just visible beneath his collar opening. "Speaking of facts and figures, thanks for bailing me out when Basht started lobbing pan-fried rocks into our laps. I'm amazed you even bothered reading all that stuff, let alone memorized it."

"I am a poet-warrior of the K'da," Draycos reminded him. "The gathering of military information is part of my profession."

"Yeah, maybe," Jack said suspiciously. "Let me guess: you made up a little song about the Edge's expeditions. Right?"

There was a short pause, and then the dragon's voice rose in gentle melody from beneath his shirt. "On Eagles' Rock two hundred strong, where humans fight a Trin-trang throng," the dragon sang. "Eight hundred fight at Sunright here: Agri and seven friend Shamshir."

Jack rolled his eyes. "Words fail me."

"Thank you," Draycos said dryly. "There are thirty more verses if you would care to hear them."

"Some other time."

They walked in silence a few more steps. "I trust you realize," Draycos said at last, "that this is a trap."

"Oh, I know," Jack assured him. "Let's hear your take on it."

"They know that someone tried to break into their system last night," the dragon said. "They suspect it was you, but are not certain. They therefore offer you the chance to learn their access codes, in the hope that you will try again tonight."

"Not bad," Jack said. "You're getting better at this sneaky stuff."

"I will take that as a compliment," Draycos said gravely. "Thank you."

"You're welcome," Jack said. "Only one thing. Unless they also think I'm dumber than dirt soup, they know I won't try another midnight stroll. Not with them alerted like this."

"What then *do* they expect?"

"I figure there are two possibilities," Jack said. "One, that I'll go straight off the chutzpah meter and try to break into the records while Basht is standing right there teaching me how to do it."

"What is a chutzpah meter?"

"Chutzpah is sheer, blatant nerve," Jack growled. Having to stop every third sentence to explain something was starting to get really old. The minute they were back on the *Essenay,* he promised himself, he was going to sit the dragon in front of a dictionary and not let him get up until he'd memorized it. "The classic definition is a kid on trial for murdering both parents, who pleads for mercy on the grounds that he's an orphan."

"An interesting term," Draycos said thoughtfully. "An equally interesting concept. What is the other possibility?"

"That I'll wait until we get to Sunright and try to tap into the computer at the outpost they're sending us to."

"Will an outpost computer have the information on the Djinn-90 fighters that we seek?"

"I don't know," Jack said. "I hope so, since that's mostly what I *am* planning to do."

" 'Mostly'?"

"Right," Jack said, smiling tightly. "You see, they'll figure they can just put a watchdog program on the computers before I arrive. That way, the minute I try to break in, they'll have me."

"But you will instead be using your special access system?"

"Actually, we can do even better than that," Jack told him. "The local Edge group will have to have a mainframe set up somewhere, and it certainly won't be off at some little observation outpost."

"It will be in their main encampment."

"Right," Jack agreed. "And since the outpost computer has to be able to talk to that one, it'll need a transmission pathway. And unless they went to the trouble of stringing a cable out into the middle of nowhere, that means a radio link."

Draycos stirred suddenly on his skin. "The *Essenay*."

"Bingo," Jack said, nodding. "Once I give Uncle Virge the access codes, he can tap into the signal and pull up whatever the mainframe has on Djinn-90 fighters. And since I won't have used the outpost computer to do it, they won't be able to trace it back to me."

Draycos was silent a moment. "That will require us to travel to Sunright," he pointed out. "You will be entering a combat zone."

"That *is* the downside to this whole thing," Jack admitted. "What do you know about observation outposts? Do they get attacked much?"

"That depends on the situation," Draycos said. "If the outpost is not considered a danger, it may be left alone as a ranging marker for artillery attacks."

"And if it *is* considered a danger?"

"It will be destroyed," Draycos said. "As quickly as possible."

Jack grimaced. "I suppose eavesdropping on the other side's communications would fall into that second category?"

"Correct," Draycos said. "Assuming the other side is aware of it."

"Figures." Jack sighed. "Okay. So the goal is to get there, pull the records, and disappear before the Shamshir figure it out."

"If they have not done so already," Draycos warned. "Perhaps it would be better to leave now and try a different group."

For a long moment Jack was sorely tempted. He already had his comm clip handy, hidden at his waist beneath his shirt. He could just keep walking until they reached the perimeter, jump the fence, and have Uncle Virge and the *Essenay* in and out before the Edge even knew what had happened.

Then it would be out to another mercenary group, one that wasn't already suspicious of him like the Edge was. He had enough fake IDs aboard the ship to try a dozen of them if he had to.

But he'd already invested six days here, not to mention the time they'd spent getting to Carrion in the first place. And time was definitely something they couldn't afford to waste. "No," he said, trying to feel like he really meant it. "We've come this far. Let's see it through."

"You do this for my people," Draycos said quietly. "Once again, I am in your debt."

"Yeah, well, I wouldn't start writing checks just yet if I were you," Jack warned.

"Pardon?"

Jack closed his eyes. "Skip it."

CHAPTER 10

Four days later, the recruits graduated.

Jack had never been through a graduation ceremony before. Of course, he'd never been in a school before, either. All of his formal education had been given to him aboard the *Essenay,* with Uncle Virgil more or less presiding over the procedure.

He would have laid good odds, though, that this graduation was vastly different from most.

The ceremony didn't last very long, for one thing. Grisko and the other drill sergeants got the recruits into formation and ran them through a few maneuvers in front of a small group of officers in full dress uniform. Colonel Elkor and Lieutenant Basht were among them, but Jack didn't recognize any of the others.

After the maneuvers, they all stood at attention while Elkor gave a speech. A short speech, fortunately, mostly consisting of telling them how lucky they were to be members of the Whinyard's Edge and how proud the Whinyard's Edge was to have them. After that, Lieutenant Basht read off the squad and platoon listings, told them they would be leaving camp at oh-seven-hundred the next morning, and ordered them to fall out.

And after that, the sergeants loaded their new mercenaries aboard transports and flew them to a nearby town for a party.

"A curious ritual," Draycos commented as Jack headed toward the restroom for his third time. "But is not alcohol a depressant to your people?"

"Sure is," Jack confirmed, looking around as he pushed his way past the groups of brand-new Edgemen crowding the tavern. Most of them were already half drunk, either laughing and staggering or else passed out on the tables where they sat. A few were huddled in corners, looking miserable, probably trying not to throw up. "I don't know why Grisko and the others are even putting up with this, let along encouraging it."

Draycos remained silent until Jack reached the privacy and relative quiet of the restroom. "There is no deep mystery to their actions," the dragon said. "The children are drinking alcohol to pretend they have become adults. The officers allow it because they believe the experience will bond the members of each platoon together."

Jack snorted. "Mostly what it'll do is make them feel lousy," he said. "Not a single one of these kids has any idea what they're doing. Probably the first time any of them has even tasted the stuff."

"Unlike you?"

Jack shrugged. "Uncle Virgil taught me to drink in case I ever had to do it for some con scheme," he told the dragon. "And right after he did, he told me to never even look at the stuff if I didn't absolutely have to. In case you hadn't noticed, I'm still on my first beer, and I've only finished half of that. Mostly, I've been drinking water."

"I had noticed," Draycos said. "I see that in some areas Uncle Virgil did indeed have good judgment."

"What Uncle Virgil had was a well-developed survival instinct," Jack said as he dug under his shirt and pulled out his comm clip. "In our business even a little fog in the brain could be fatal. Fogged reflexes, too. I never knew when we might have to drop everything and make a run for the tall grass."

He took a deep breath as he lifted the comm clip. "Uncle Virge isn't going to like this," he warned.

Uncle Virge didn't. "This is not the deal we made, Jack lad," the computer growled. "Not the deal at all."

"You don't hear me doing cartwheels of joy either, do you?" Jack asked. "There just isn't any other way."

"Of course there is," Uncle Virge said, suddenly gone all soothing and persuasive. "Look, lad, it's over. I know you've done your best. But the hand's been lost, the jackpot's been taken off the table, and it's time to face reality. You and your poet-warrior friend have no choice but to take this to the StarForce."

"We've been through this, Uncle Virge," Jack reminded him. "It isn't safe for Draycos to show himself around."

"But it's safe for him to drag you into a war zone?" Uncle Virge countered. "Besides, if Draycos gets himself killed, what happens to his people?"

"I will not be killed," Draycos said calmly. "Nor will I allow Jack to be harmed."

"Big promises," Uncle Virge huffed. "How exactly do you intend to make amends if you're wrong? A signed apology from the grave?"

"I'm not going to argue with you," Jack cut him off. He was nervous enough without bringing up the subject of graves. "We're going, and that's that. You want to hear the plan, or don't you?"

"Go ahead," Uncle Virge muttered, sulking now.

Jack laid it out for him. Uncle Virge was not impressed. "*That's* the plan?" he demanded scornfully. "That house of buttered toast is the best our poet-warrior can come up with? No wonder his people are losing their war."

Jack winced, not daring to look down at Draycos. "Yes, that's it," he told Uncle Virge stubbornly. "The only question is whether we do it on our own or whether you come along to help. Well?"

"Of course I'll help," Uncle Virge muttered, back to sulking again. "You know where you'll be?"

"It's the Edge's November Six outpost," Jack told him. "According to the map they showed us, it's just to the south of Bear Mountain in the southwestern part of the Gray Hills. Can you pull up a map?"

"Yes," Uncle Virge said. "Yes, I have it."

"Basht said we'd be flying into a major Parprin town called Mer'seb," Jack told him. "From there, our squad will take a transport up to November Six. I'm guessing Mer'seb is where the Edge's HQ and mainframe computer are, but you'll need to check on that. Got it?"

"Of course," Uncle Virge said.

"Okay," Jack said. "Incidentally, you weren't by any chance poking around the training camp last—let's see—last Tuesday night, were you?"

"Certainly not," Uncle Virge said. "I'm right here in the spaceport where you left me. Why?"

"Just wondering," Jack said. "There was a something off by the fence that night that had the patrols stirred up for awhile, that's all."

"Did it cause you any trouble?"

"Actually, it did us a favor," Jack said. "That's what opened up the grounds and gave us a clear run at the HQ building."

"Where you weren't able to get what we needed," Uncle Virge said pointedly. "Which is why we're going with this other lunatic plan. Some favor."

Jack felt his lip twitch. "I suppose."

"But I suppose we're stuck with it now," Uncle Virge went on. "I don't suppose you happen to know where the actual battle lines are drawn on Sunright?"

Jack glanced down at Draycos, got a sideways slide of the head in return. "Not a clue," he said. "But we should be able to figure it out once we see which direction the shots are coming from."

"Not funny, Jack lad," Uncle Virge said darkly.

He had a point. "Sorry," Jack apologized.

"'With tired arms,'" Draycos murmured, "'and eyes fatigued, the soldiers stood to mark the deed.'"

"That isn't funny, either," Uncle Virge growled.

"Sorry for both of us, in that case," Jack said, frowning

down at Draycos. What had that been all about? "I have to go. We'll see you on Sunright."

He clicked off the comm clip and tucked it away again inside his shirt. "Well, he's not happy," he commented. "But he didn't go completely frantic on us, either. That's a good sign."

"Or else he merely recognizes he has no choice but to obey."

"Maybe," Jack conceded. "What was that 'tired arms' thing you said to him?"

"It was part of a poem," Draycos said. "I have been working on translating my poetry into your language. I often recite parts of it to Uncle Virge late at night, while you sleep."

Jack had to grin at that. Uncle Virgil had always despised poetry, which meant that the computerized Uncle Virge probably did, too. "I'll bet he just loves that. So what part didn't he think was funny?"

"It was a poem about the Battle of Chatii," Draycos said, his voice low and grim. "There the K'da and Shontine held a bridge against the Valahgua while a group of alien civilians escaped behind them. What the warriors did not know was that some of the civilians had been turned by the enemy, and soon they were being attacked from both sides."

Jack winced. "I can see why he didn't like it. Did they all—I mean . . . die?"

"Actually, most of them escaped safely," Draycos said. "It was your comment about not knowing where the battle lines were drawn that brought that part of our war to my mind. So it was not Uncle Virge near the camp that night."

"I guess not," Jack said. "I hadn't really thought he would have been that careless, anyway."

"Which returns us to the question of what *did* stir up the patrols," Draycos pointed out.

"I don't know," Jack said. "Maybe they were just jumping at shadows."

"Trained soldiers usually do not do that."

"I suppose." Jack looked down at the dragon's head beneath his shirt. "By the way, I want to apologize for what Uncle Virge said about your people losing their war."

"No apology is necessary," the dragon said calmly. "I understand his motivation. Having failed to argue us out of our plan, he was attempting to shame us out of it."

"Ah," Jack said. Yes, that was definitely something from Uncle Virgil's old bag of tricks. "Anyway, I'm sorry. I'm glad you didn't take offense."

"I did not say I did not take offense," Draycos said. His voice was still calm, but there was a thin layer of ice on it. "I merely said I understood. Either way, though, the fault is not yours."

Jack swallowed. "Okay," was all he could think of to say. "Well. Let's get back to the party."

The transports left the camp at precisely oh-seven-hundred the next morning, bright and shiny and efficient.

Unfortunately, the same could not be said of their passengers.

Most of them, to quote one of Uncle Virgil's favorite phrases, looked like death warmed over and stuck to the pan. Most were pale and limp, some looked like they'd just done a twenty-mile hike, and a few were practically sleepwalking as they stumbled aboard the transports.

Amid such company, Jack knew, someone as fresh and un-hungover as he was would be a little too noticeable. He picked a role somewhere in the middle of the spectrum, hanging his head as he shuffled along. Occasionally, he made sure to bump into the person on either side of him.

The transfer to the various spacecraft that were waiting for them an hour later wasn't much better, but at least no one got accidentally left behind. As far as Jack ever heard, none of them fogged their way aboard the wrong ship, either.

The trip to Sunright took seven days. Tango Five Zulu was one of three squads from their training group going to this particular world. Sergeant Grisko and Lieutenant Basht were along, too, though Basht made it clear he would only be staying long enough to write up a report on the current situation there.

There were also two hundred regular Whinyard's Edge mercenaries aboard, heading in to reinforce the eight hundred troops already there.

The numbers struck Jack as rather ominous. A twenty-five percent increase in ground forces meant the Edge was either making a major push for victory or scrambling madly to avoid defeat.

Either way, it was likely there was going to be shooting. Possibly a lot of it.

Starting with the second day of the flight, after everyone had recovered from their hangovers, Basht had Tango Five Zulu start their equipment preparation. They now had the actual fold-top computers they would be taking up to November Six with them, and it took the better part of two days to load the various codes and data onto them from the ship's main system.

The rest of the time was spent practicing the computer drills they'd learned back on Carrion. They would continue practicing, Basht declared several times, until they were able to run them in their sleep.

Jack wasn't sure they ever got *that* good at it. But he had to admit that Basht pushed them at least halfway there. By the time they reached Sunright, the whole squad was dreaming about the drills.

Finally, yet all too soon, they had arrived.

The town of Mer'seb was nestled into a narrow river valley, its tightly packed buildings surrounded by tall, thickly forested hills. A slow river wound lazily through the center of town from the east, taking a sharp southern turn a half mile or so beyond the western edges.

Between the town and the river curve was a large area of mostly flat stone. It was on this natural landing pad that the Whinyard's Edge spaceship set down.

The adult Edgemen had obviously been through this routine before. They lined up at the airlock hatchway in full combat gear, rifles and machine guns slung for marching.

When the hatch opened, they strode out and down the ramp, forming quickly into six-man ranks. Marching in step, they headed into the city along a typically Parprin straight-as-an-arrow street. At Grisko's direction, the three teenage squads fell in at the back end of the column.

"Well, this is fun," Jommy muttered under his breath from beside Jack as they marched past the first row of houses at the edge of town. "They planning to walk us the whole way to the outpost?"

"Probably just to the main Edge HQ," Alison said from Jommy's other side. "It's on the far side of town."

"How do you know where it is?" Jommy asked suspiciously.

"I saw the flag from the top of the ramp," she said mildly. "You really need to pay more attention to details, Randolph."

Jommy muttered something inaudible under his breath. "Oh, come on," she chided him. "Frost up, okay? It can't be more than a mile or two."

"Yeah, but what's the point?" he growled.

"They're probably showing us off," Alison said. "Look at the people."

Keeping his face forward as he'd been taught, Jack threw a sideways glance at the Parprins lining the street. Quite a few of them had come out to see the parade, all right. Mostly females and their children, though there were also a few of the taller males mixed in.

He frowned, taking a second look. The thin Parprin face always seemed sad to him; but these Parprins looked even sadder than usual. The children huddled close by their mothers, and the males tended to stand in groups of two or three, talking softly together. "They don't look very happy to see us," he pointed out quietly.

"Maybe they don't know we're here to help them," Jommy muttered sarcastically.

"Or maybe they think this whole thing has gotten out of hand," Alison suggested slowly. "Maybe they don't think their mine is worth all this."

"Isn't worth what?" Jommy scoffed. "Defending from poachers?"

"Not worth completely scrambling their lives for," Alison countered. "My father used to say that lawyers and soldiers came out of the same expensive box. If you couldn't settle things without them, you weren't going to like what it cost to settle things with them."

Jommy grunted. "Your dad must have been a real kick to grow up with."

Alison didn't answer.

They continued on in silence. Jack kept his eyes moving, wishing he knew how to read Parprin faces better. Maybe he was only imagining their discomfort.

Still, he couldn't shake the feeling that they looked like people watching an occupying army march through their town.

They reached an area of three- and four-story buildings, obviously the town's main business district. Here the females and their children were replaced by Parprin males, many of them wearing the brightly colored robes of shopkeepers or the only slightly drabber sparkle-cloth of businessmen. There were also quite a few aliens of different species represented in the crowd, and even an occasional human. Apparently, Mer'seb was a trading center for many of the alien enclaves and colonies scattered around this region of the planet.

Again, it seemed to Jack that a lot of the Parprins were whispering together as the mercenaries marched past. The rest stood in silence, watching the procession. The other aliens, in contrast, mostly glanced at the spectacle and then moved on. No one cheered or waved.

"I got it," Jommy said suddenly. "They just don't realize it's a parade, that's all. We should have brought a brass band with us."

"That's funny," Alison said scornfully. "Personally, I was just thinking about how much I was enjoying the silence."

And at that instant, almost as if on cue, the silence of the crowd was abruptly broken. From all around them, the city erupted in noise: the distant thunder of small rockets, the closer rattle of machine gun fire, the shouts and screams of the injured and the dying and the terrified.

The Whinyard's Edge was under attack.

CHAPTER 11

The chatter of gunshots filled the air. The deeper, slower rhythm of heavier weaponry and small explosions added counterpoint, the noise echoing from the sides of the buildings. The entire column of soldiers was under attack.

And like the raw recruit that he was, Jack just stood there in the middle of it.

"Move!" Draycos snarled, his whole body aching for action. An attack. Soldiers being shot at and probably killed where they stood. Civilians possibly caught in the line of fire, with nowhere to escape to.

And he, a poet-warrior of the K'da, lying uselessly in two-dimensional form against Jack's skin.

It was a horrible situation. A horrible, shameful situation. For a K'da warrior in the midst of combat to sit idly by, not lifting a claw to help, was a violation of all he'd ever stood for.

But he had no choice. To move now, to give in to the urge to defend and protect, would doom the K'da and Shontine to ultimate destruction.

Because if the unknown enemies who had slaughtered his advance party ever learned that someone had survived, they would hunt him down like a newborn cub. And when he died, the last chance to warn the refugee fleet would be gone.

But even as his frustration rose like poison in his throat, Jack finally freed himself from his stunned paralysis. "What do I do?" he hissed, breaking into a run toward the edge of the street.

"Find cover," Draycos told him. Sliding along Jack's body, he got a claw beneath the collar of the boy's shirt and popped open the sealing seam. Bad enough being trapped here unable to help, without being mostly blind, too. He ran the claw down far enough to open the shirt to midchest and peered out.

It was about as bad a place to be caught in an ambush as he could have asked for. All around them, medium-tall buildings provided high ground for the attackers, and they were taking full advantage of it. A cloud of drifting smoke was starting to collect overhead by the rooftops, and he could see muzzle flashes from several windows. Most of the attack seemed to be coming from three buildings: the three-story structure next to the building Jack was heading toward, plus the two four-story ones across the street from it.

He could also see now that the city was surrounded by forested hills. More high ground, probably the source of the deeper and more distant sounds of heavy weapons. The enemy had planned their attack well.

There was a jarring thud as Jack reached the building and slammed hard into the wall beside a large decorative planter with a red-blue bush sprouting out of it. "I don't think I like this," the boy muttered in a shaky voice as he fumbled his

Gompers flash rifle off his shoulder and dropped into a squat beside the planter. "How in—?"

He broke off as an angry face suddenly filled Draycos's field of view.

The K'da froze in place. But the Whinyard's Edge mercenary wasn't interested in dragon tattoos just then. "Gimme that," he barked, snatching the rifle from Jack's grip. Holding it across his chest, he took off to the left.

"Oh, that's terrific," Jack muttered, curling into a tight ball behind the planter. "Now what?"

Draycos raised his head from Jack's skin far enough to press an eye through the open gap in his shirt, and caught a glimpse of the mercenary as he disappeared around the corner of the building. The man's own machine gun, he noted, was still bouncing against his back. "He wanted a long-range weapon to use against the hillside attackers," he decided. "His own weapon is for closer work."

"Right," Jack groused, curling up a little tighter. "Like there isn't enough to shoot at *here*."

He had a point. Gunfire was pouring down from the three buildings Draycos had already identified as being held by the enemy. The Edgemen were returning fire, but they were pinned down and mostly without cover. Even as he watched, three of them tried to charge the door of one of the buildings, only to be scattered back by a peppering of small explosions.

Fortunately, most of the civilians seemed to have vanished. Some had ducked into walkways and alleys or else had taken refuge inside buildings not held by the enemy. Those outside the immediate battle zone were running in all directions, their brightly colored outfits bouncing like flowers in a stiff wind.

And then, as Draycos looked over the top of the planter, his eyes caught a horrible sight. Three Parprins, one tall and two very short, were huddled together in obvious terror against the side of Jack's building. A mother and her cubs, trapped in the middle of the firefight. "There," he said urgently. "Civilians."

"What?" Jack asked, not moving a muscle.

"Civilians," Draycos repeated, lifting a claw through the open shirt and pointing.

Reluctantly, Jack untucked his head far enough to throw a quick glance over the planter. "Okay, yeah, I see them."

"Stop merely seeing and give them aid," Draycos snapped. "Get them to cover."

"What? *Look,* Draycos—"

"Do not argue!" Draycos cut him off.

Small objects were starting to rain down from the enemy buildings' rooftops now, objects that exploded on impact. Popcorn bombs, he remembered them being called in Jack's mercenary manual, thrown by something called a popcorn machine. The three Parprins huddled even tighter together in response, the mother wrapping her arms protectively around her cubs. "You are a soldier," Draycos said. "The job of a soldier is to protect those in danger. Now, *protect* them."

"How?" Jack demanded, sounding scared and miserable. "I can't even protect myself. What do you want me to do?"

Draycos leaned out from Jack's shirt as far as he dared. On the far side of the planter, between Jack and the Parprins, was a set of steps leading upward into an alcove. He couldn't be certain at his angle, but it looked like the alcove led up into a doorway. "That opening to your right," he told Jack. "Move them in there. It may be a doorway that will allow you into the building. If it is not, it will at least provide cover from the popcorn bombs."

Jack shook his head. "I can't," he said. "It's too far."

A shot slammed into the far side of the planter, nearly toppling it over onto Jack. The boy jerked, then curled even more tightly around himself. "Listen to me," Draycos said, keeping his voice quiet and steady. "The enemy is not trying to shoot civilians. If they were, those three would already be dead. We may assume they will therefore not deliberately shoot at you if you are merely trying to help them."

Jack shivered. "But if no one's shooting at them, why should I do anything?"

"Because a random shot may still find them if they stay where they are," Draycos said. "And because it is your duty."

Beneath him, he felt Jack's muscles tense. "All right," the boy said, taking a deep breath. He hunched his shoulders, taking another careful look over the top of the planter.

And then, so suddenly it startled even Draycos, he was on his feet, running a zigzag path toward the Parprins.

Draycos had just enough time to flatten himself onto Jack's skin before they were there. "Come on," Jack urged, tugging at the mother's arm. "Come on. We've got to get inside."

For a second the Parprin female just stared blankly up at him. Jack tugged at her arm again, pointing toward the stairs and the alcove.

Then, just as suddenly as Jack had made his decision, the mother made hers. Scrambling upright, she grabbed her cubs' hands and raced toward the alcove.

Jack stayed right behind them until they reached the steps. Then, bounding up past them as they climbed, he pushed the door open and hurried them inside.

The room they found themselves in took up the entire front of the building. Small round tables were laid out in what seemed to be a random pattern, with tiny colored disks neatly arranged on them. The windows were large, facing onto the street and also to both sides. None of them had curtains or barriers of any sort.

Near the center of the room was a wide staircase leading up to the second floor, with a set of curved metal railings on both sides. "Make them sit beside the staircase," Draycos whispered to Jack. "It will give some protection from fire through the windows."

"I should be out there," Jack muttered as he herded the Parprins to the side of the stairway. "I should be out helping them."

"You cannot," Draycos told him firmly. "You have no weapon. You can only stay here and guard the civilians."

"But those are supposed to be my comrades out there," Jack insisted. "You're the one who's always talking about duty. How can I just sit here while they're getting shot at?"

"You cannot help them," Draycos repeated, flicking his

tongue out once through the gap in Jack's shirt. The smell of Parprin wasn't one he had tasted before, and he made a mental note of its texture. "But I can. And I will."

Jack exhaled in a huff. "Okay," he said. "Be careful."

He helped the Parprins down with their backs against the stairway wall; and as he did so, he lifted his left hand over the top of the railing.

Draycos was out of the sleeve in an instant, leaping onto the stairs. With his scales tingling, his battle senses fully alert, he headed up.

CHAPTER 12

The second floor was much like the first: wide spaces, tables with merchandise, no cover near the windows. Draycos didn't pause, but continued up the next stairway to the third floor.

There he found what he was looking for. This floor, instead of being devoted to merchandise, had been divided by low partitions into an orderly maze of small office-like areas. Even better, the windows were partially covered by thick, decorative drapes. Keeping to the cover of the partitions, he made his way to one of the side windows and looked cautiously out.

The side of the next building was perhaps ten feet away, an easy leap for a K'da warrior. He scanned all the windows, but there was no one in sight. Apparently, the attackers were concentrating on the street side, where the Edgemen were pinned down.

Still, they hadn't completely neglected their defense of this side. Between the two buildings a steady trickle of popcorn bombs was raining down.

It was an interesting defensive method, one which the K'da and Shontine had never used. The popcorn bombs were propelled outward from a central launcher somewhere on top of the building. As each bomb cleared the edge of the roof, it sprouted a small parachute, which stopped its outward motion and turned it instead to fall straight down. The parachute then popped off, sending the bomb falling at normal speed toward the street below.

For a few seconds Draycos watched the bombs, studying their pattern. With the proper timing, it should be cub's play to get though it.

The rooftop was a little ways above his position as he looked out the window, and he couldn't see if there was anyone up there tending the popcorn machine. Still, the Edge manual had said such devices ran automatically, so it had probably been left on its own. He would have to risk it.

He looked down, and felt his jaws crack open in a tight smile. Whatever else the popcorn bombs were supposed to do, they were also having an unintended but useful side effect. Just as the gunfire from the windows was creating a hazy smoke screen around the tops of the buildings, so too the bombs were creating a smoky mist of their own at ground level.

Which meant that, when he made his move, neither the attackers nor the defenders would see a thing.

He pushed open the window and backed up to midway across the room. There he crouched low, watching the bombs fall past the window. He could feel the blood pounding through his body, pouring oxygen and nutrients into his muscles in preparation for the effort ahead. Out of the edge of his eye he could see the golden color in his scales turn to black as some of the extra blood flow trickled into them.

The K'da warrior was ready.

Across the room, the pattern of falling bombs reached the proper point. Digging his claws into the carpet, he charged.

A quick sprint took him back to the window. He jumped up to the sill with his front paws, got his rear paws planted on the sill behind them, and leaped up and outward.

There was no time to wonder what would happen if he had made a mistake in the pattern. Fortunately, he hadn't. His jump took him sailing cleanly through a gap in the artificial hailstorm and landed him on top of the low parapet around the edge of the roof.

The popcorn machine had been set up near the center of the roof, spitting its deadly dispatches toward and over the edges. As Draycos had expected, there was no one tending it. Staying low beneath the stream of bombs, he sprinted across the roof.

This particular machine was slightly different from the one that had been shown in Jack's manual. But it was similar enough. Two quick slashes through the power and control cables, and the rain of bombs stopped.

Beside the machine was a trap door leading down into the building. Prying open the popcorn machine's magazine, he pulled out two of the small bombs. Then, ready to toss them in if necessary, he pulled the trap door open a crack.

He flicked his tongue into the gap. There was an alien tang in the air, almost buried beneath the taste of the explosive powder of the guns. The taste of Parprin was there, too, but faint and stale, plus the stronger scent of a human. Neither the human nor alien scents seemed to be nearby.

He lifted the trap door the rest of the way up. Below was a narrow stairway leading down to a door that had been propped open. No one was visible, and the enemy did not seem to have set any alarms or booby traps. Tucking his two popcorn bombs out of the way beneath his forearms, he headed down.

The open door below led into the center of a corridor lined with ten doors. Apartments, he decided, or possibly private offices. Silently, he prowled down the hallway, listening and tasting at each door.

At the second and fourth doors to the left, on the side facing the street, he found the enemy.

He took a moment to lay the two bombs on the hallway floor by the fourth door, where the door would strike them if it was opened carelessly. Then, returning to the second door, he pulled it open.

The attacker's setup was again something he'd seen in Jack's manual. At the window sat a slender, long-barreled weapon on a tripod, angled sharply downward to fire at the street. A belt of ammunition ran up to it from a small suitcase on the floor.

The gunner himself was of a species Draycos hadn't met before: short and stocky, with large ears and clumps of feathers poking out of a mottled red-and-purple skin. His heavy battle vest had a shoulder patch showing a long, curved sword, and his scent matched the alien smell Draycos had tasted by the trap door.

He was seated cross-legged in the center of the room, well back from the window, leaning comfortably against the front corner of a large desk. With the help of a small video monitor in one hand and a control stick in the other, he was firing the weapon by remote control.

Foolishly enough, he was sitting with his back to the door. Perhaps he assumed his large ears would warn him of any intruders.

Draycos didn't give him the chance to correct that error. A single leap across the room landed him behind the alien. A single slap of his forepaw bounced the other's head against the desk and sent him sprawling unconscious onto the floor.

For a moment Draycos crouched beside him, listening to the rhythm of his breathing. The soldier was alive, but definitely out of the fight.

One room down. One more room to go, and then he would have done all he could. He turned back to the door.

And paused as a sudden thought struck him. Perhaps he wasn't quite finished here yet.

He spent a minute learning how to work the control stick. Then, manipulating the buttons and wheels delicately with his claws, he raised the muzzle of the gun to point at the building across the street. Studying the monitor, he located one of the windows where a similar gun was firing down into the street.

Smiling to himself, he lined up the crosshairs on the other gun and fired.

The result was all he could have hoped for. His bullets hammered into the other weapon, shaking it like a puppet with tangled strings and toppling it back out of sight. Swinging the gun to the right, he found the next enemy weapon and again opened fire. This gun was sturdier, and it took him two bursts to knock it out of action.

He swung the gun toward the next building over, aware that his time was rapidly running out. If the operators of the two ruined weapons were quick and smart, they would alert the soldier two rooms away from him that this weapon had fallen into enemy hands. The soldier would then come and try to take it back.

The enemy was definitely smart, and even a little quicker than Draycos had expected. From down the corridor came a pair of sharp cracks as the two popcorn bombs he'd left behind the other door went off.

The enemy was coming.

He took another two seconds to ruin one more enemy weapon, then dropped the control stick and loped back toward the door. Leaping up, twisting to the side in midair, he landed with a gentle thud against the wall just above the door. His claws dug into the hard wood and held on.

Just in time. Beneath him, the door was pulled violently open, and a burst of gunfire spattered across the empty space.

Seeing no one but his unconscious comrade, the soldier shifted his aim toward the desk, the only reasonable hiding place in the room. The bullets slammed into the wood, sending clouds of splinters flying. It was just as well, Draycos decided as he gazed down, that he hadn't tried to hide there.

The gunfire stopped, and a human soldier eased cautiously into the doorway, his gun held ready. Unhooking one paw from the wall, Draycos leaned over and slapped hard at the side of the man's head.

This one was tougher than his alien comrade had been. The blow sent him staggering to the side, but he managed to stay on his feet. He shook his head once, as if to clear it, just in time to catch the slap of Draycos's tail as it struck him in the same spot where the first blow had landed. The man toppled to the floor, his gun clattering out of his grip, and stayed down.

Draycos slipped out of the room and headed back toward the stairway. The hallway was empty, but he knew it wouldn't be for long. Already he could hear several pairs of footsteps moving upward from the floor below. Either more of the attackers were coming to investigate, or an advance party of Whinyard's Edge defenders was on its way.

Either way, his time had run out. He reached the stairway and climbed toward the roof, noticing as he did so that all the gunfire outside seemed to have ceased.

And as he eased his head up through the trap door, he found out why. In the distance, heading toward them at high speed, were three small aircraft.

So the Whinyard's Edge had finally called in air support. About time.

He raced across the roof, hoping Jack was still where he'd left him. He reached the edge, and in a single move leaped up onto the parapet and then threw himself into a flat dive toward the window he'd originally left.

His jump was slightly off, and his paws fumbled a bit as he ducked in through the window. Regaining his balance, he retraced his steps through the partitions and back to the wide stairway.

He made his way down to the second floor landing. There he paused, listening. The three Parprins were talking quietly, and from the direction of their tense voices he could tell they were still sitting or standing at the bottom of the stairway.

Unfortunately, Jack was keeping quiet. Had he moved away somewhere? If so, there might be a problem getting back to him without the Parprins seeing him.

And if he didn't move quickly, the Parprins would be the least of his worries. With much of the attack broken, and the aircraft dealing with the rest, he could see through the windows that the Edgemen were beginning to move purposefully around in the street. One of their first tasks, he knew, would be to check the nearby buildings for enemies.

All the buildings. Including this one.

He focused his attention on the stairway railing. A metal railing; and metal, he knew, conducted sound quite well. Reaching up, he gave it three gentle scratches with his claws.

To his relief, there was an immediate answering scratch.

He lifted his head carefully, just far enough to see. Jack had one hand resting on the railing, the fingers beckoning impatiently.

Slinking down the stairs, Draycos reached the spot where Jack stood. He touched the boy's hand and slid quickly up his sleeve as he changed into two-dimensional form. Shifting along Jack's skin, he worked his way around into his accustomed position.

Just in time. Across the room, the door slammed open. Moving carefully, Draycos peeked out through Jack's shirt.

Sergeant Grisko stood framed in the doorway, a small machine gun held high across his chest. Behind him, Draycos could see Alison Kayna and Jommy Randolph.

"There he is," Jommy said, pointing past Grisko's shoulder. "I told you."

"Yeah, you sure did." Grisko leveled the full power of his glare at Jack. "And what the frinking rip," he demanded, "are you doing *here?*"

CHAPTER 13

Quickly, Jack got his hand down off the railing and stiffened to attention. "I was moving these civilians out of danger, sir," he explained, giving a short nod toward the Parprins still huddled on the floor beside him. "They were caught in the fire zone."

"Very commendable," Grisko said tartly. If he was pleased with Jack's answer, it didn't show on his face. "Anyone give you any actual orders to that effect? Or did you dream it up on your own?"

"And then decide to hide in here with them?" Jommy muttered.

"Shut up, Randolph," Grisko snapped, his eyes never leaving Jack's face. "Someone give you orders, Montana? *Anyone* give you orders, Montana?"

"Not exactly, sir," Jack admitted, feeling a fresh batch of sweat breaking out on his forehead. This was just great. He'd survived an enemy attack; and now he was going to catch it from his own side?

And possibly catch it even worse than just being shot at. The manual had listed some pretty severe penalties for desertion under fire. "There wasn't anyone nearby to give me any orders," he went on, trying desperately to think his way out of this.

"The manual lists twelve standing orders for behavior in a firefight," Grisko ground out. "You remember any of them being to turn tail and run like a rabbit?"

Jack clamped down on his tongue. "No, sir," he conceded. Beside him, one of the Parprins whimpered.

And at last, inspiration. "But I *do* remember that an Edgeman's primary job is service to our employer," he continued more confidently. "Since our employer on Sunright is a Parprin group, I assume all local Parprins come under that heading."

"Nice try," Grisko said. "Problem is, the protection of civilians comes three points *below* support of your comrades on the list."

Beside him, Alison stirred. "I wonder where his gun is," she murmured.

Grisko frowned, his eyes flicking to Jack's shoulder and then glancing at the floor and tables around him. "That's a good question. You got a good answer?"

Jack would have smiled with relief if he'd dared. Of course; the escape hatch he'd been trying to find. "One of the other Edgemen took it, sir," he said.

A slight frown creased Grisko's forehead. "Why?"

"I believe he wanted to use it against the snipers up in the hillside," Jack explained. "All he was carrying was a Heckler-Colt MP-50. Not really suitable for long-range work."

"So why didn't he give you his H-C?" Grisko demanded.

"I didn't have time to ask him, sir," Jack said. "He just

took my Gompers and ran with it. To be honest," he added with what he hoped was just the right touch of humility, "I don't think the regulars think very much of us as combat soldiers."

Grisko's lip twisted. "I can't really say I blame them." He looked at the Parprins, back at Jack. "All right, get outside," he growled. "We're forming up. Go get your Gompers back, then get your carcass into position."

He turned sharply and stalked outside. Jommy gave Jack a dark look, then strode out behind him. "I guess we don't get to see a court-martial, after all," Alison remarked. "Too bad. Might have been interesting."

"Sorry to disappoint you," Jack said, waving a farewell to the Parprins and heading toward the door. "At least you got to watch me squirm. Was that enough entertainment for one afternoon?"

She lifted her eyebrows. "Hey, I got you off the hook. What more do you want?"

"You could have mentioned a little earlier that you saw that thug-ugly take my gun," Jack pointed out stiffly.

"Yes, I could have said something earlier," Alison agreed. "But why should I?"

"Maybe because Grisko was getting himself worked up into a real froth about this?" Jack suggested as he stepped up to her. "By the time you actually spoke up, there was half a chance he wouldn't have even cared anymore that I hadn't had a gun. He would have been ready to nail me to the wall right there. Ever think of that?"

"Sure," she agreed. "And maybe if I *had* said something

right off the top, he'd have thought I was just covering for a deserter. Then we'd *both* have been for the hot seat. Ever think of *that*?"

Jack frowned, his annoyance fading a little as he gazed into her eyes. There was something odd there, simmering beneath the surface like a churning of molten rock.

Anger, and frustration, and determination. And perhaps more than a little fear.

A lot like the way he'd been feeling lately himself. For about the last year, in fact, ever since Uncle Virgil had died.

"I thought we were comrades in arms," he said quietly.

She regarded him coolly. "I don't stick my neck out for you, Montana," she said, just as quietly. "You or anyone else."

Turning, she walked out the door. "Okay," Jack muttered aloud to himself. "Good to have that settled."

"An interesting person," Draycos murmured from his shoulder.

"Oh, yeah," Jack said sourly. "Interesting like a rare and delicate tropical disease. Come on, let's go find the clown who's got my gun."

It took several minutes for Jack to track down the man who'd taken his flash rifle. It took several more to actually get the weapon back. Still eyeing the hillside suspiciously, the soldier was clearly not interested in giving up his long-range firing capability, and told Jack so in language that would have made Grisko proud.

But by then the officers were starting to call the troops back into formation, and Jack's mention of Grisko's name also seemed to carry a certain amount of weight. Eventually, with one last muttered curse, the soldier shoved the Gompers back into Jack's hands and stomped back to rejoin the column. On Draycos's advice, Jack replaced the half-used clip with a fresh one, then hurried back to his own place in line. A few minutes later, the whole group resumed their march through town.

But not with nearly the brash confidence they'd shown earlier. Now, they marched with their attention turned upward, toward the windows and rooftops as they passed beneath them. Their weapons were again slung over their shoulders, but it seemed to Jack that none of them let his or her hand get too far from the trigger. And, of course, the combat aircraft floating watchfully overhead were a continual reminder of what had just happened.

The Whinyard's Edge had gotten its nose bloodied today.

There was a change in the townspeople, too. Not surprisingly, the crowds that had been lining the street earlier were gone. Those who found themselves near the marching soldiers seemed intent on hurrying to be somewhere else.

Earlier, the people had seemed nervous and uncertain. Now, they were flat-out afraid.

Mentally, Jack shook his head. Whatever result the Edge commanders had hoped for with this stroll through the city, he was pretty sure that wasn't it.

They reached the headquarters compound without any

further trouble. A pair of carriers loaded with their equipment rumbled in behind them, and there was a sort of confused chaos as footlockers and other gear were sorted out.

Back on Carrion, Jack had gotten the impression that his squad would be staying in Mer'seb for a few days before moving up to the November Six observation post. But barely an hour after their arrival, the order came down for eight of the new squads to assemble immediately for transport to their field destinations. Tango Five Zulu was one of them.

They boarded their transport, a Lynx Personnel Carrier, in the courtyard of the HQ compound. Along with Tango Five Zulu, two squads of regular Edgemen would also be traveling to November Six. Sergeant Grisko was along, too, at least long enough to help them set up.

The Lynx was a good-sized transport, designed to haul at least three times the number of people they had on this trip. That meant some elbow room for a change, and Jack took quick advantage of the situation by staking out a pair of seats in the back next to one of the small windows. Setting his pack down on one of the seats, he strapped himself into the other. If he kept his eyes glued to the scenery, maybe he could pretend he was heading out on some sort of vacation.

On a vacation, and not into a war zone.

It turned out to be a futile hope. Unlike the other Edge transports Jack had traveled on so far, the Lynx actually looked like a military vehicle. Intruding constantly on his view of the landscape were the muzzles of two large-caliber machine guns poking out from under one of the stubby wings. The wing itself was painted in a camouflage pattern designed to help it blend in while on the ground.

The landscape itself wasn't all that exciting, either. The hilly ground around Mer'seb soon gave way to a short stretch of plains and small lakes, then began to turn hilly again. Grisko had said the trip to November Six would take two hours, and Jack found himself wondering just how big the territory was that this handful of Edgemen was supposed to be protecting.

With such cheery thoughts dancing around his brain, he huddled over with his forehead against the cold plastic of the window and drifted to sleep.

He awoke suddenly, startled by a light jab on his wrist. He snapped his eyes open and looked around.

No one was leaning intently over him. For that matter, no one was paying any attention to him at all. The nearest other person, Rogan Mbusu, was sprawled limply two seats over, snoring quietly to himself. Outside the window, the afternoon sunlight was throwing long shadows across the ground.

The light jab came again; and this time, Jack recognized it as the touch of a dragon's claw. The signal of a dragon's nagging. "What?" he muttered toward his shoulder.

"I must speak with you," Draycos murmured back.

"Now?"

"Now."

Jack glared down at his shoulder, a wasted effect with his shirt and jacket mostly in the way. Draycos had a real gift for rotten timing.

But there was nothing to do but go along. Unstrapping, he headed past the equipment storage area to one of the tiny restrooms in the far rear of the transport. He closed the door, sealed it, and did a quick check for monitors. There weren't any. "This had better be good," he warned as he closed the toilet lid and sat down.

With the usual sudden surge of weight, Draycos popped out of Jack's collar. He landed on the area around the sink and turned around, balancing himself there with apparent ease. "It is important," he promised. "Do you remember the map we were shown of the area around November Six?"

Jack frowned. "You woke me from a good nap for *this?* A geography quiz?"

"Please," Draycos said earnestly. "The Gray Hills flow from northeast to southwest, with Bear Mountain to the north of the base. Correct?"

"Right," Jack said. "Then the Gray Hills continue down toward Octrani Lake, with the Partanra River flowing out mostly west from there."

"While a tributary of that same river is the water that flows through Mer'seb," Draycos said. "The Parprin town we have just left. Correct?"

"Sounds right," Jack confirmed, stifling a yawn. "So what?"

"So this," Draycos said. "The place we were shown on the map is not the place we are going."

CHAPTER 14

Jack sat up straight, his tiredness suddenly gone. "How do you know?"

"I am a poet-warrior of the K'da," Draycos reminded him. "The reading of maps is part of my profession. I have been watching the ground through the window."

Jack's stomach was trying to do somersaults. "How far off are we?"

"Our course from Mer'seb should have taken us at an angle slightly north of east," Draycos said. "We did indeed set out in that direction. But approximately one hour ago we changed gradually to a more northerly direction."

Jack glanced at his watch. They'd been in the air about an hour and a half. Thirty more minutes until landing.

Or at least, that was what Grisko had told them. Maybe the sergeant didn't know something had gone weird, either.

Then again, maybe he did. "So where *are* we headed?"

"If we are still to land in one half hour, I believe we will arrive near the western edge of the Gray Hills," Draycos said. "Perhaps three hundred miles north of November Six."

"And if we *don't* stop in half an hour?"

"All regions beyond that are either neutral or considered enemy-controlled."

Jack chewed at his lip. Terrific. "So what do we do?"

"There are two squads of fully armed soldiers aboard," Draycos reminded him. "They could be made aware of the situation."

The dragon had a point. If the pilot was an enemy agent trying to take them to the wrong place, two squads of Edgemen ought to be able to argue the point with him. Surely none of *them* wanted to end their trip in enemy territory, either.

On the other hand, having a gun battle in the middle of a flying transport didn't sound like a very smart idea. "I'd better talk to Grisko," he decided. "Come on, get aboard."

Obediently, the dragon stepped onto Jack's outstretched hand and slithered up his sleeve. Sealing the neck of his shirt again, Jack headed out.

Grisko was sitting alone in the back, on the opposite side of the Lynx from Jack's seat. He'd probably picked that spot so he could watch the rest of the group.

Though at the moment he wasn't watching anything at all. His eyes were closed, his head sagging slightly against the headrest.

Jack pursed his lips. The sergeant was probably not going to like this. "Sergeant Grisko?" he said quietly.

Grisko's eyes remained closed. "What is it, Montana?"

"I think we're off course, sir."

Grisko pried one eye open and squinted up at him. "Excuse me?"

"We're not headed for November Six," Jack told him. "We seem to be going somewhere north of there."

Grisko pried the other eye open, and for a long moment he seemed to be studying Jack's face. "Good observation," he said at last. "As it happens, our orders have been changed. The Shamshir moved their transmitter yesterday to point Kilo Seven. We're moving with it."

"Oh," Jack said. So that was it. All nice and simple and reasonable. Certainly a lot less threatening than a daring mid-air hijacking.

Which left only one little problem. Uncle Virge was still heading for the area around November Six, which meant that Jack's plan for getting the Djinn-90 information was no longer going to work. Worse, when it came time to wrap this up and make a run for the tall grass, his primary escape route was going to be sitting on the ground three hundred miles away.

Grisko was still gazing up at him. "Is this a problem for you?" he asked.

"No, sir," Jack said, trying to sound as unconcerned as possible. "Sorry to have wakened you."

"Half an hour to the base," Grisko said, closing his eyes again. "Better get some rest. I've got a strange feeling you're going to be on sentry duty tonight."

Jack grimaced. "Yes, sir."

He returned to his seat and curled up again beside the window. Even in the few minutes he'd been away the shadows of the trees had visibly lengthened along the ground. Sunset couldn't be too far away.

"I do not like it," Draycos murmured from his shoulder as he slid open the neck of Jack's shirt again.

"Me, neither," Jack agreed. He pulled his shirt open a little more and shifted in his seat so that the dragon would have a better view out the window. "You first."

"I am not familiar with your transmission science," the dragon said. "But with the K'da and Shontine, a device that can reach between stars is large and not easily moved. Certainly not in a single day."

"That's mostly true here, too," Jack agreed. "The *Essenay*'s got a compact InterWorld transmitter built into it, but Uncle Virgil was always setting up deals and scams across the Orion Arm. He couldn't risk having them traced back to him through a commercial InterWorld site."

"Even our largest ships cannot carry such a transmitter," Draycos said. "Are such common here?"

"Not really," Jack said, frowning. "Actually, not at all. The biggest StarForce ships have them, I know, and I'm pretty sure a few starliners do, too. But now that I think about it, I can't remember anyone else in Uncle Virgil's circle having one aboard their ships. Whatever he paid for ours, the price must have been astronomical." He snorted. "Either that, or he stole it."

"Then let us assume the Shamshir transmitter is not easily portable," Draycos said. "Moving it would cost them considerable time and effort. It would not be an operation they could hide."

Jack nodded. He and Draycos were definitely thinking along the same lines. "In other words, it should have taken a couple of weeks to get a new site prepared, break down the transmitter, and then move it. Which means we should have heard about this before we left Carrion."

"Correct," Draycos said. "And if they only began moving it yesterday, there would be no need for us to travel there tonight."

"We could have hung around Mer'seb for a few days while they got it set up."

"Correct," Draycos said. "That may imply the Shamshir are aware of our interest and are trying to keep us from succeeding. But it may also imply there is something else about this mission that we are not being told."

"Could be." Jack scratched his cheek. "Though I suppose there could be a simpler explanation."

"Which is?"

"That the Shamshir simply changed their minds about where to put their transmitter," Jack said. "And no one bothered to tell any of us about it until now."

"But timely information is vital to a warrior's job," the dragon objected. "Surely they would not hold it back from us."

"Hey, I'm just a raw recruit," Jack said. "Remember? Nobody has to tell *me* anything."

"Talking to the window?" a familiar voice asked pleasantly from behind his shoulder.

Jack clamped down on his tongue as he felt Draycos slide quickly back to his usual position. "Hello, Alison," he said, turning to face her. "Sure. Doesn't everybody?"

"Don't tell me," she said. She plucked his pack from the

seat beside him, dropped it unceremoniously onto the floor, and sat down. "Let me guess. You were staring at the window because you needed a moment to reflect."

Jack made a face. "That was pathetic. I hope you didn't come all the way over here just for that."

"No, mostly I wanted to see what the view was like out there," she said, craning her neck to look past him. "And to find out what you and Grisko were talking about."

Jack felt his eyes narrowing. "What do you mean?"

She gave him a patient look. "You. Grisko. Talk. Two minutes ago. You need me to spell any of the words for you?"

"No, I've got it, thank you," Jack growled. "Not that it's any of your immediate business, but we were discussing the fact that we're not going to November Six. We're going to Kilo Seven instead."

It was Alison's turn for narrowed eyes. "Why?"

"According to Grisko, the Shamshir moved their transmitter."

For a brief moment he thought he could see an echo of the emotional swirl in her eyes that he'd noticed once before. But then she just nodded. "Oh," she said.

" 'Oh'?" he repeated. "That's all? Just 'oh'?"

"What more is there?" she countered reasonably. "If the transmitter's been moved, we move with it."

He shrugged. "I suppose."

She tilted her head, her eyes shifting down from his face to his chest. "So that's what they're all talking about, huh?"

Jack frowned. "What?"

She nodded toward his chest. "Your dragon tattoo. Nice."

Jack looked down. Sure enough, part of Draycos's jaw was visible through the partially open shirt. "Oh, it's lots nicer than that," he assured her, putting a little boasting into his tone. "It goes all the way around, and then some. See?"

He pulled the collar a little to the side to reveal more of the dragon's face. The last thing he really wanted to do was advertise Draycos's presence this way, and he was pretty sure Draycos felt the same way. But he'd met enough men with tattoos to know you didn't get one with the idea of hiding it. Alison was pretty sharp, and if he didn't brag about his dragon, she might wonder why. "Here—the head's the best part," he went on, reaching for the shirt's sealing seam. "Let me get this open a little more—"

"No, that's all right," Alison said hastily. "Really. I was just wondering if it was like the one the Dragonbacks wore."

"I already told you I never heard of the Dragonbacks until a month ago."

"Maybe *you* didn't," she pointed out. "But your tattoo artist might have."

"Oh." That angle hadn't occurred to him. "Is it?"

"Is it what? Oh." Alison shook her head. "Not even close. The Dragonbacks had their tattoos between their shoulder-blades, just below the neck. A little dragon, coiled around itself into a circle. Nowhere near as big as yours."

"You seem to know a lot about them."

She shrugged. "Like I said, I do my research. Always terrific to talk to you."

She got up and headed back forward to her own seat. "Interesting," Draycos murmured.

"What is?" Jack asked, turning back to the window. "Her obsession with dragon tattoos?"

"That she noticed your conversation with Sergeant Grisko and wondered about it," Draycos said. "She is quite observant."

Jack closed his shirt down to where it had been before Alison showed up. "Observant *and* nosy," he agreed. "I wonder if they know this is her second try at joining a mercenary group."

"I do not know," Draycos said. "Do you think you should tell them?"

Jack gazed out the window, weighing his options. Below them, the shadows were lengthening still more. Above them, the sky was definitely beginning to darken. "No," he decided at last. "But let's keep an eye on her."

The last twenty miles were spent traveling at treetop height, with the Lynx dodging its way around the handful of taller trees and an occasional hill or tall rock.

Jack gazed out at the blur of green shooting past his window, fully expecting to crash and burn any minute. Uncle Virge could have pulled off this kind of maneuver easily. But it wasn't Uncle Virge running the controls up there.

Fortunately, the pilot knew what he was doing. He ran the course without so much as a single serious bump, and a few minutes later had set them down in a small clearing at the base of a rocky cliff face.

If parts of the Carrion training base had been spartan, the

Kilo Seven outpost was downright primitive. The only solid structure was a flimsy looking prefab building about the size of a one-bedroom hotel room. Grisko identified it as the outpost HQ, and the place where Tango Five Zulu would be setting up their computers and listening gear.

The rest of the outpost consisted of four tents scattered beneath the trees. Two of them looked like sleeping quarters for the soldiers, with the other two probably serving as mess tent and storage facility. To the west, downslope from the rest of the camp, was the distinctive narrow tent of a latrine.

Further out, to the north and south of the camp, Jack spotted two small defensive positions. They weren't much, little more than foxholes with a couple of long gun muzzles poking out. Still, it was nice to know that the enemy couldn't overrun the place without the Edge at least being able to put up a fight.

The sun was down by the time they left the Lynx. The mercenaries set to work immediately, unloading their gear and taking it to their assigned tents. Jommy and the rest of Tango Five Zulu were also busy, lugging their computers and other equipment to the headquarters building.

Jack, to his complete lack of surprise, found himself assigned to night sentry duty.

His post was about sixty yards south of the camp, perhaps forty yards beyond the defensive foxhole on that side. All sixty yards of it were downhill. "Here's your cage," Grisko said, stopping beside a tree that looked rather like an elm with a bad skin condition.

"Cage?"

"Your sentry post," Grisko said with exaggerated patience. "Didn't you read the manual?"

"I must have missed that part," Jack murmured. He *had* read the manual, thank you, and there had been no mention of the term "cage" being used for a sentry post.

But there was nothing to gain by pointing that out. He'd apparently been put on sentry duty for waking up Grisko aboard the transport. He didn't really want to see what would happen if he added to his crimes by arguing with the man.

"Well, then, pay attention now," Grisko growled. He pointed to a group of four small round monitors that had been nailed to the tree trunk. Each of the monitors showed a slightly fuzzy image, and each had a control stick embedded in the trunk beneath it. "There's your Argus system. You *do* remember Argus systems, don't you?"

"Yes, sir," Jack said, more confidently this time. Argus was a passive observation system for sending images from one area to another. The far end, called the eye, could be up to five hundred feet away, with a fiber-optic cable linking it to one of the monitors here at the sentry post. The direction each viewer was pointing could be shifted by means of a wire control system. The control line ran through its own cable alongside the fiber-optic one, connecting to the lever beneath the monitor.

Jack could remember thinking when he first read about it that Argus had to be the most ridiculously primitive system in the known universe. It was only later, as he read about electronics and power-source detectors, that he had realized there was actually a good reason for the system. Out here in the middle of a forest, the electronics of a normal sensor system would stand out like a nightlight in a dark room. Argus, on the other hand, would never even be noticed unless the enemy happened to trip over one of the cables.

"Yeah, I'll bet you do," Grisko grunted. Reaching to a small rectangular plate beneath the monitors, he flipped up its protective cover. Underneath was a glow-in-the-dark schematic of the area, with Jack's outpost in the middle and the edge of the main camp behind him along the bottom. "Here's where your eyes are located," he said, tapping the map in four places. "You'll be relieved at midnight. *Don't* fall asleep."

He turned back toward the camp. "What if there's trouble?" Jack asked.

Grisko frowned. "Like what?"

"Like the enemy shows up," Jack said. "Do I get a comm clip or something to call in an alarm?"

Grisko was looking at him as if he was crazy. "Don't be absurd," he said. "The enemy doesn't even know we're here."

"But—"

"Tell you what," Grisko cut him off. "If they come this way, you haul out your Gompers and start shooting. We'll notice. Trust me."

With that he stalked off into the growing darkness, the matting of dead leaves crunching under his feet. He disappeared from sight, leaving only the sound of his footsteps to mark where he was. A dozen seconds later, even those had faded into silence.

And Jack and Draycos were alone.

CHAPTER 15

Jack had never liked the woods. He'd never much liked the outdoors in general, for that matter. Nearly all of his life had been spent in cities or spaceports, or in spaceships like the *Essenay*. Places with bright lights, and people, and no strange noises.

Occasionally when he and Uncle Virgil had been running a scam, they'd had to spend time in someone's country estate or mountain retreat. But at least there they'd mostly been inside at night. Nature had been something beyond the walls, safely out of view.

His last brush with nature had been on Iota Klestis a month and a half ago. He'd taken a few short trips outside the ship, mostly during the day but once or twice at night. That was how bored and restless he'd been.

But at least there he'd had the comforting bulk of the *Essenay* at his back, and Uncle Virge's watchful eye on the surrounding terrain.

Uncle Virge.

He stared out into the woods, an all-too-familiar pang of uncertainty and loss and fear whispering through him. The first time he'd felt it was back when he was three years old and finally realized that his parents weren't coming back to him. He'd felt it again a year ago at Uncle Virgil's death, when he'd suddenly found himself alone in the universe with nothing but a computerized personality to look after him.

Now, here in the darkness of the night, he was feeling it for a third time. Because whatever happened with Draycos, he knew down deep that his relationship with Uncle Virge had been changed forever.

The thought was as frightening and alien as the dark woods around him. Up to the time when he'd met Draycos, Jack's life had been fairly simple and more or less comfortable. For all the annoyances inherent in Uncle Virge's personality, the computer really was mostly easy to get along with.

More to the point, he was the only friend Jack had.

The strange noises of nature were beginning to whisper through the darkness around him. Mostly insects and small animals, he guessed, with an occasional bird or bat-like something flapping past overhead. Up above the trees he could still see the sky, but here at ground level it was already night.

And then, suddenly, something big and heavy landed on the back of his neck.

He jerked away with a gasp, his hand reaching automatically to swat it away, even as he realized it was just Draycos popping out from his jacket collar. "Geez!" he hissed. "Don't *do* that."

"Do not do what?" Draycos asked, landing on the leaves beside him with a soft crunch.

"Never mind," Jack growled, feeling like an idiot. "You startled me, that's all."

The dragon cocked his head. "You do not like it out here," he declared.

Jack snorted. "No kidding, Sherlock."

"Pardon?"

"Skip it." Shaking away the introspective thoughts, Jack stepped over to the Argus monitors for a closer look. There were two filters on each, he saw, either of which could be slid over the image. Experimentally, he tried one.

The image didn't change much. He tried the other, and suddenly, the darkness was pockmarked with scattered bits of light. "Ah-ha," he said, feeling about as pleased as he could under the circumstances. "That's the infrared. The other one must be deep UV."

"Pardon?"

" 'UV' is short for ultraviolet," Jack explained, sliding the infrared filters over the rest of the monitors. "It's a kind of light we can't see directly, but there are some species and some kinds of equipment that show up real well with it."

"And infrared?"

"Infrared is heat," Jack told him, peering at each of the monitors in turn. Nothing but small animals and birds, at least as far as he could see. "Anything warm gives that off. Those thugs who were looking for us back on Vagran were using IR detectors. Back when we were hiding out on that Wistawki balcony, remember?"

"Yes," Draycos said. "I was somewhat surprised at the time that they did not locate us."

Jack shrugged. "You probably don't look like anything anyone's ever seen before. Matter of fact, you might not even look alive—we'd have to do a heat profile on you to know for sure. Either way, I guarantee you don't look like a human."

"That could be useful."

"It already has been," Jack pointed out.

"True." Draycos studied the monitors. "The images are not very clear."

"They sure aren't," Jack agreed. "I guess that's the best you can do without electronics and power sources."

The dragon hopped up onto a nearby stump and craned his neck. "Perhaps I should explore the perimeter."

"Oh, no," Jack said quickly. "Forget it. You just stay put, right here."

Draycos twisted his head around to look back at him. "You do not need to be afraid, Jack," he said, his voice low and soothing. "I am a poet-warrior of the K'da. I will protect you."

"I appreciate your confidence," Jack said. "But Good Intention Highway isn't one I want to travel just yet."

The tip of Draycos's tail twitched. "Do you refer to the saying, 'The road to hell is paved with good intentions'?"

Jack frowned. "Yeah. Where did you hear that?"

"Uncle Virge quoted it to me," the dragon said. From his stump he jumped up onto the side of one of the trees and clung there by his claws, gazing out into the night.

"During one of your late-night poetry sessions?"

"Yes. He has many such sayings with which to illustrate his points."

Jack felt his mouth twist. "Let me guess. His main point is that he wants you to go away and leave us alone."

"That is the core of it," Draycos confirmed. "He does not feel that the survival of my people should be any concern of yours."

Somewhere ahead, a twig suddenly snapped. Jack jerked, snatching up his Gompers and pointing it into the darkness. "Do not be afraid," Draycos assured him quickly. "It was merely a small animal obtaining a meal."

Jack lowered the flash rifle, letting his breath out silently. "Okay," he said.

Draycos pushed off the tree trunk and dropped back down to Jack's side. "I do not understand your fear," he said, looking up at Jack's face. "I would have thought that in your previous profession you must have faced danger many times."

"Not like this," Jack said, shaking his head. "I was always a kid before. Even when we were breaking into bank vaults, I knew the police weren't going to shoot unless I pointed a gun at them or tried to get away."

He plucked at a fold of his uniform jacket. "Here, it's all different. Here, I'm a target. Not because I'm breaking any laws, but because I'm wearing this uniform. *Just* because I'm wearing this uniform."

"That is the way of the soldier," Draycos reminded him. "Part of your task is to draw danger away from the weak and powerless."

Jack snorted. "Just what I always wanted."

Draycos cocked his head. "It is an honorable profession, Jack."

"Maybe where *you* come from it is," Jack retorted.

"It is not so here?"

"How would I know?" Jack sighed. "All right, yeah, I suppose it is," he conceded. "At least most of the time. But we sure don't seem very popular here on Sunright."

"I do not understand."

"You saw the people on the march through town today," Jack said. "Well, no, probably you didn't. The point is that they weren't exactly cheering us on."

"One does not usually cheer in the middle of an attack."

"This was before the attack," Jack told him. "They were just staring at us, watching us march. Like we were invaders instead of protectors." He snorted. "*After* the attack, it was even worse. Then, they were afraid to even get near us."

Draycos was silent a moment. "You are mercenaries, not regular soldiers," he pointed out. "Perhaps that is the difference."

"Maybe," Jack said. "I don't know. But according to Uncle Virge's history lessons, people sometimes treated regular soldiers the same way when they were in a war the people didn't like."

"That is wrong," Draycos said firmly. "The soldiers deserve the respect and honor of the people they defend. If the war is wrong or misguided, the people's objections should be directed at the leaders."

"Hey, I'm just telling you how it is," Jack said. "I don't write the history, I just report it."

"I understand," Draycos murmured.

He hopped up onto his stump again, peering off into the night. Jack found himself studying the dragon's silhouette, a black shadow against a slightly lighter background. "It was different for you, wasn't it?" he asked. "I mean, your people were fighting for their lives. That must make a difference."

"It does," Draycos agreed. "There were still objections at times, of course, but they were settled by the leaders."

"Pretty quickly, I'd guess," Jack said. "Did all of you have to become warriors?"

"All had to have soldiers' training," Draycos said. His voice was soft and oddly distant. "Those who did not serve directly were required to fill support positions. There was no other way."

"I suppose," Jack said. So when Draycos called himself a poet-warrior it wasn't really that big a deal? Or was it maybe the poet part he was so proud of? "So basically any K'da can do what you do?"

The dragon seemed to draw himself up. "Not at all," he said stiffly. "All indeed can become soldiers. But not all are warriors."

Jack frowned. "What's the difference?"

"A warrior of the K'da is a special person," Draycos explained, and there was no mistaking the pride in his voice. "He or she has certain inborn talents and abilities, plus the desire to turn those talents in the direction of protecting the K'da people. We are found at an early age, and offered this position."

The tip of his tail twitched. "No, Jack. One without poetic talent may be able to make two sentences rhyme on occasion. But you would not call him a poet, with the true gift of poetry. So is the difference between soldier and warrior."

Jack nodded. He'd tried writing a poem once, back when he was ten. The result had been pretty pitiful. "So how old were you when they started your training?" he asked. "You said once you were younger than I was when you had your first battle."

"That is true," Draycos acknowledged. "I was not yet a warrior at that time, though, but was still in training. My full training lasted nearly four years."

"Four *years*?"

"Yes," the dragon said. "Though I was of course a soldier during much of that time. We could not afford for warriors-in-training to merely be students during a war for survival."

"Yeah," Jack murmured. Four years, compared to the ten days he'd just gone through. "I guess I must seem pretty pathetic to you. I'm barely even a soldier, let alone a warrior."

"You do as well as your abilities allow," Draycos said diplomatically. "Your talents lie in other areas."

"Right," Jack said with a sigh. "And I bet you'd trade three of me right now for a single good soldier."

"Perhaps that could be arranged," the dragon suggested dryly. "Shall I go get Alison?"

Jack glared at him, a waste of effort in the darkness. "Very funny."

From behind them came the faint sound of lifters. "There goes the Lynx," Jack commented, turning to look.

But nothing could be seen though the trees. The sound changed pitch as the transport shifted to horizontal motion and headed away from the camp. Jack looked up, trying to catch a glimpse of it through the trees. Again, nothing. "Could you tell which direction it was headed?"

"From the sound, it appeared to be traveling southwest," the dragon said.

"Back to Mer'seb," Jack said. Somehow, the sound of the departing shuttle made the darkness out here seem a little deeper. "Well, good luck to them. They're sure not going to find a welcome carpet spread out."

"Do you refer to the citizens?" Draycos asked. "Or do you expect another Shamshir attack?"

"I was talking about the people," Jack said. "But as long as you've brought it up, I did overhear Lieutenant Basht telling someone they'd found two Shamshir mercenaries in one of the buildings. They'd been knocked cold, but weren't hurt otherwise. Your handiwork?"

"Yes," Draycos said. "The tides of warfare flowed to my advantage."

"Whatever," Jack said. "How come you didn't kill them?"

The dragon's tail arched. "There was no need. I wished merely to halt their attack. That I did."

"Yeah, but they'd already killed about ten Edgemen," Jack pointed out. "I thought you didn't approve of killers."

"I do not approve of murderers," Draycos corrected. "There is a difference between murder and warfare."

"That's not what some of our people say," Jack told him.

This was, he realized dimly, a pretty stupid argument to be having at a time like this. Especially out here, with him wearing a soldier's uniform and carrying a soldier's gun.

But there was something about the darkness and the noises that was making him unusually talkative tonight.

Or maybe it was the silence between the noises that he was trying to fill. "There are people—a lot of people—who think warfare is just the government's way of—"

"Quiet!" Draycos cut him off. He twisted his head away from Jack, his pointed ears suddenly standing straight up.

For a second, Jack stared past him into the darkness. There was nothing out there he could see. Then, suddenly, his brain caught up with him, and he turned instead to the Argus monitors.

The dragon was right. Something had moved into view on one of the monitors. The image was fuzzy, but it definitely had the basic shape of a human being, and it was moving toward the camp.

Moving toward Jack.

He flipped up the schematic showing where the Argus eyes were positioned, his pulse thudding hard in his neck. Okay; this was Eye Number Three. That was *there*; which meant the figure coming toward him must be *there* . . .

He didn't realize Draycos had moved to his side until the dragon spoke. "They are approaching," he murmured, his breath warm on Jack's ear.

Jack's pulse picked up speed. *"They?"* he muttered back. "There's more than one?"

The dragon's tongue flicked out at one of the other monitors. "There," he said. "And there," he added, pointing to another.

Jack gripped his flash rifle like he was trying to squeeze it in half. There were two more figures, all right, half hidden behind rocks or trees. Even as he focused on one of them, it moved away from its hiding place and crossed quickly to another one. "How many are there?" he asked.

There was no answer. "Draycos?" he repeated, twisting around.

The dragon was gone.

"Draycos!" he called as loudly as he dared, his eyes darting around the darkness. The K'da had vanished, all right. Probably gone ahead to check on the intruders.

Jack hissed between his teeth. Suddenly, he felt very exposed out here, standing in the faint glow from the Argus monitors. He stepped away from them as quietly as he could, cringing every time his feet crunched into the leaves.

A few feet away was the tree stump Draycos had been perched on earlier. He dropped down behind it, clutching the flash rifle as if his life depended on it. Which it probably did.

All right, Jack, calm down, he told himself sternly. Three of them wasn't too bad, if that was all there were. It could be just a quiet scouting party, with none of them actually looking for a fight.

If that was all there were. He looked over his shoulder at the Argus monitors, but here at the stump he was too far away to see them clearly. What he needed was to be over there watching the monitors, with Draycos nearby to protect his back.

Except Draycos was off who knew where. Doing who knew what.

Blast the dragon, anyway. Of all the times for him to run off and play soldier.

And then, from somewhere ahead, somewhere very close ahead, came the soft sound of a footstep.

CHAPTER 16

Jack froze in place, hardly daring to breathe. *Draycos?* was his first, hopeful thought.

But no. The dragon was a lot quieter than that.

There was another footstep, and another pause. Jack stared into the darkness, straining so hard his eyeballs hurt. In the faint light from the stars overhead the forest was little more than a jumble of dark gray shadows crisscrossed by even darker black ones.

The sound came again.

He had it placed now. It was just behind a tall bush about ten feet directly ahead of his stump.

Had the intruder spotted him? That was the big question. It didn't seem likely to Jack that he would still be moving forward if he had. After all, he had no way of knowing that the sentry on duty was a scared fourteen-year-old with ten whole days of combat training under his belt.

Unless the one behind the bush was only a decoy. Unless his job was to deliberately make enough noise to draw Jack's attention while someone off to the side leisurely lined up a rifle on him.

Jack crouched a little lower behind the stump, trying hard

to become part of the decaying wood. It was a useless attempt for someone shaking as badly as he was. Carefully, he eased his flash rifle around to point toward the bush.

Now what?

Sure, he could fire. But if this one was only a decoy, the shot would show them exactly where he was. In that case, Jack himself probably wouldn't live long enough to even see the first guy hit the ground.

But if he *didn't* shoot, and this one was out there alone . . .

Draycos! he thought desperately toward the woods. *Where are you? I need you!*

Where *was* the blasted dragon, anyway?

There was another footstep. Swallowing hard, Jack got his finger on the trigger.

And suddenly, an animal the size of a large frog came hopping out from behind the bush.

Jack's breath went out in a silent whoosh, every muscle in his body suddenly turning to jelly. The frog jumped again, its landing sounding exactly like a cautious human footstep.

He really, *really* didn't like the woods.

A flicker of motion caught the corner of his eye. He glanced up—

And twitched violently as Draycos dropped into a crouch at his side. "You're going to give me a heart attack yet," he growled at the dragon. "I swear—"

"Quiet," Draycos bit out. "They are coming. You must retreat."

Jack's muscles went tight again. "There are more than three of them?"

"There are eight," Draycos said. "All wear the shoulder emblem of the Shamshir. You must warn the others."

Jack felt cold all over as he stared frantically into the night. Three of them might have been a scouting party. Eight of them meant an attack.

And attackers, he knew, always started by silencing the sentries.

He jerked as Draycos's snout jabbed impatiently into his ribs. "What?" he gasped.

"Did you not hear me?" Draycos demanded. "I said you must warn the others."

"I can't," Jack hissed. "They didn't give me a comm clip."

"I know that," Draycos said, his voice impatient. "You must leave here and go to them."

Jack shuddered. The thought of eight guns pointed at his back . . . "I can't," he said. "I'll never make it."

Draycos lifted his head to the level of Jack's face. The bright green eyes bored into his face, the tip of the long snout nearly touching his nose. "Listen to me, Jack," the dragon said. "They are coming. They are not yet close enough to harm you. But they soon will be if you do not leave. You must go *now*."

Jack peered out into the shadows. Draycos was right, he knew.

But his legs still refused to move.

Because what if the dragon was wrong? What if he'd missed one or two of the enemy on his scouting trip? What if there was someone right now hiding in the trees, waiting for him to give away his position?

"Jack?"

Jack clenched his teeth together. No, the dragon was right. He'd been in this same kind of situation before with Uncle Virgil. If he just sat here, sooner or later he would lose by default.

Besides, how much more conspicuous could he be than sitting here with a bright, gold-scaled dragon standing beside him?

"Okay," he breathed. Slowly, cautiously, he stood up into a crouch and backed away from the stump.

No one shot at him. He kept backing up, passing the Argus monitors. Draycos stayed by the stump, his tail arched, his ears pointed skyward as he listened. Jack reached the first group of trees and passed between them.

Only then did Draycos turn and bound silently toward him. He reached Jack's side, then stopped and turned around. "Keep moving," he ordered, his ears lifting again. "I will guard you from any approach."

Jack kept going, walking as quickly as he dared. The night seemed alive around him, and he could feel a thousand hidden eyes staring in his direction. Three more times along the way Draycos caught up with him, and each time then stayed behind as guard. Wishing fervently he'd listened to Uncle Virge and come up with a better way to trace those blasted Djinn-90 pursuit fighters, Jack kept moving.

There was no one manning the defense position on this side of the camp. For a moment, as he passed the foxhole, Jack was tempted to jump in. He could activate the weapons there and spray the woods behind him with gunfire. *That* ought to discourage the Shamshir soldiers.

But he was only tempted for a moment. It might discourage them, but it might also start them shooting back at him. The longer he could put that off, the better.

Especially if he could get someone else to do both the shooting and the being shot at. Directly ahead was one of the big tents, the ones he'd decided earlier were sleeping quarters. Panting a little from the long uphill climb, he stumbled to the door and pulled it open.

It was a sleeping tent, all right. There were twelve sets of bunk beds arranged around a small table with four matching chairs. The chairs were empty.

So were all the bunks.

For a long moment Jack just stood there staring. Twelve bunk beds. Twenty-four beds. All empty.

All of them?

All of them.

He stumbled back outside, to find Draycos lurking beside the corner of the tent. "You did not alert them?" the dragon asked.

"There isn't anyone to alert," Jack told him tightly. "They're gone."

The dragon's long neck arched back. "Gone? Gone where?"

"How should I know?" Jack countered, looking around the encampment. Everything was dark and silent.

Everyone asleep, he had thought. Now, he wondered if anyone was even here.

"Shall we try the other tent?" Draycos asked.

"Let's try the HQ first," Jack said. "It's on the way, and the rest of the squad should still be setting up."

"Yes," Draycos agreed. He leaped up to Jack's shoulder and disappeared down the back of his neck. "Hurry. The Shamshir are still approaching."

With its windows shielded, the headquarters building was as dark as the rest of the camp. But as Jack approached, he saw to his relief that there was a narrow sliver of soft light coming from under the door. At least someone was home there.

Unless the rest of Tango Five Zulu had carelessly left the lights on before they vanished into the night with everyone else. Mentally crossing his fingers, he pulled open the door.

The rest of Tango Five Zulu hadn't vanished. They were all still there, kneeling in a circle in the center of the room, their faces bowed toward the floor, their hands clasped behind their necks. Two men in full nighttime camouflage outfits were standing behind them, their weapons leveled at their backs.

But Jack only saw that out of the corner of his eye. His full attention was on the other two men in the room, standing beside the squad's stack of fold-top computers.

Their guns pointed directly at Jack.

CHAPTER 17

"Walk inside," a hard, flat voice growled from somewhere to his right. "No noise."

Carefully, trying not to make anything that looked like a suspicious move, Jack turned his head that direction.

Standing in the corner of the room, positioned where he could guard the doorway Jack was still standing in, was a Brummga.

Jack stared at the wide alien, his mouth dropping open a little. Suddenly, it was like he'd gone back in time to the ruins of the *Havenseeker* and his first meeting with Draycos.

But this Brummga wasn't wearing the same mismatched collection of clothing and combat gear. He was dressed in the same camouflage outfit as the other Shamshir mercenaries, with the same curved-sword patch on his shoulder. And the gun he was holding was smaller and sleeker than the shiny black monstrosity the other Brummga had pointed at Jack back then.

Different Brummga. Different group.

Worse situation.

The Brummga twitched his weapon, emphasizing his order. Shaking away the uncomfortable feeling of déjà vu, Jack took another step into the room. Just to prove he knew how to behave in a situation like this, he carefully closed the door behind him.

"Anyone else?" one of the men across the room asked.

Jack opened his mouth to tell him he had no idea—

"Okay," the man said. "Keep sharp."

Jack closed his mouth again. Of course; the man hadn't been asking him. He'd been talking to a spotter outside on a comm clip.

For a moment he wondered if the spotter might have caught a glimpse of Draycos. Maybe even have seen the dragon go two-dimensional and slide onto Jack's skin.

But no. If he had, he surely would have said something. And the guy in here didn't seem like he was that good of an actor.

"This the last of your tech squad?" one of the other men asked, slinging his gun over his shoulder and striding over to Jack. He had thrown back the hood of his camo jacket, and Jack could see that his head was totally bald beneath it. Like a billiard cue ball with a face painted on it, he thought irreverently.

"Yeah, that's him," Jommy said, his voice low and surly. "He was on sentry duty."

"Didn't do a very good job," Cue Ball commented, taking Jack's Gompers rifle away from him.

Jack thought about it a second and decided he wasn't going to let that one pass. "Oh, I don't know," he objected calmly. "I spotted the eight guys you've got coming in from the south."

He had the minor satisfaction of seeing Cue Ball's face flicker with surprise. "Sure you did," the other said suspiciously. "How many of them were human?"

There were five quick taps on the back of Jack's arm. "Five," Jack said. "Why? You taking inventory?"

Cue Ball snorted. "Get over there," he growled, jerking his head toward the other teens. "Join your buddies."

Jack did as he was told, crossing the room and kneeling down between Brinkster and Li. He could feel Brinkster's body trembling where her shoulder touched his. Li, on his other side, seemed in shock, as if refusing to believe this was really happening.

"Come on, you know the drill," Cue Ball prompted, jabbing Jack's own gun into the back of his neck. "Hands on your head; fingers laced together."

Again Jack obeyed, glancing around at the others. Jommy's surly tone, he could see now, hadn't been entirely honest. The kid was angry, all right, and trying hard to look brave and tough. But he was also scared. Very scared.

Eleven-year-old Rogan Mbusu wasn't even trying to put up a good front. He was crying openly, tears streaming down his cheeks, his body shaking with silent sobs. Beside him, Alison knelt without moving, her face expressionless.

Stunned by it all, like Li? Or was she simply better at burying her emotions than the others?

It was only then that he realized Alison was staring back at him. Staring very intently.

He frowned back at her. Was she trying to ask him something? Tell him something?

Concentrating on Alison, he jerked as a pair of hard hands slipped around his neck. Before he could react further, the hands were gone.

Leaving something hard and cold snugged up around his throat.

"All right, listen up," Cue Ball said. Out of the corner of his eye, Jack saw the man fasten a gray metal collar around Li's neck. "These things are called control collars." He moved on to Alison. "In case the famous Whinyard's Edge ten-day training course didn't cover them, let me explain. Their sole purpose in life is to choke the living daylights out of you if you try to run or make trouble."

He stepped behind Rogan. The kid nearly collapsed at his touch; Cue Ball merely propped him up with one hand and put on his collar with the other. "They can get triggered one of two ways," he said. "First, if you wander too far from the tether marker. One of us has that. I'm not going to tell you which one."

He slid on Jommy's collar. "The other way is for one of us to fire 'em directly. That'll happen if we decide somewhere along the way that you're not worth the trouble of taking back with us. And we're easily convinced. So don't try."

"This guy's just a bundle of charm," Jack muttered under his breath.

Cue Ball, now standing behind Brinkster, apparently had good ears. The next thing Jack knew, the big man had slapped him hard against the side of his head. "Watch your mouth, kid," he growled.

Jack grimaced. "Yes, sir," he said, trying to sound meek and subdued and feeling annoyed with himself. He'd forgotten Uncle Virgil's first rule of being a prisoner: always look as helpless and harmless as you possibly can. It tended to make the enemy overlook you.

And if there was one thing he really wanted right now it was to be overlooked.

"One more thing," Cue Ball added as he snapped Brinkster's collar around her neck. "All six of these collars are keyed together. Plus side for us: we don't have to fumble for six different buttons if we have to drop a troublemaker. Minus side for you: if one of you gets the chop, all of you do. Think about that if you're tempted to be a hero."

"We're set here, Lieutenant," one of the other men reported.

Jack glanced that direction. The men had the squad's fold-top computers packed into a couple of backpacks, and were hoisting them up onto their backs.

"Right," Cue Ball said. Lieutenant Cue Ball, rather. "We're heading out now, kiddies. Keep it nice and easy and quiet. We've got people positioned all around the camp, just like Sentry Smart Mouth here said. You whistle up an alarm, and all you'll do will be to get the rest of your buddies slaughtered in their bunks. Understood? Good."

They left the HQ building, the prisoners in single file, the Shamshir troops spread out on both sides around them. It wasn't until they were halfway across the silent encampment that Jack suddenly caught the full significance of that last comment.

Lieutenant Cue Ball had just threatened to shoot up the camp. But the threat didn't make sense, because Jack already knew that the rest of the Edgemen had disappeared.

Which meant that Lieutenant Cue Ball *didn't* know that.

He puzzled at it all the way to the empty guard post and on into the woods. Okay. So the Edgemen were gone. But the Shamshir raiders hadn't made them go away. Not by killing them, or kidnapping them, or luring them out of camp.

So where *had* they gone? And why?

He still hadn't come up with any answers by the time they met up with the eight soldiers Draycos had spotted earlier. The group was spread out near Jack's sentry cage, clearly waiting for Lieutenant Cue Ball and his prisoners to show up. A backup force, undoubtedly, in case something had gone wrong.

Jack found a minor bit of satisfaction in the fact that there were indeed five humans in the group.

They continued on down the slope. Some clouds had rolled in, cutting off most of the already dim starlight, and Jack found himself in a continual struggle with underbrush that wanted to trip him up and low-hanging tree branches that wanted to take his forehead off.

But the darkness also provided an unexpected plus. With visibility near zero, he could feel Draycos carefully probing at the collar with his claws, searching out its operation.

And then, the pressure around his neck disappeared.

The dragon had popped the collar.

Jack tensed, trying to decide which way he should jump. A second later he nearly yelped in frustration as the pressure came back again.

A very rude word flashed across his mind. But Draycos was right. Walking through the middle of an unfamiliar forest, with armed enemies all around, was not exactly the ideal spot to make a break for it.

He just hoped they would find a better opportunity before Lieutenant Cue Ball stood all of them in front of a firing squad.

Ten minutes later they reached a small clearing. An unmarked Flying Turtle 505 transport sat there, a much smaller vehicle than the Lynx the squad had arrived in earlier. It was guarded by two more Brummgas with Shamshir shoulder patches. The whole crowd piled aboard, and they headed up into the sky.

And finally Jack had it figured out. The whole thing was a clever trap, with Tango Five Zulu and their computers as the bait. They'd been sent out here to draw Lieutenant Cue Ball and his men into grabbing range. Now, as they lifted out of the woods, the hidden Edge forces would spring their trap.

Only they didn't. The Flying Turtle slid along under the cloudy sky at treetop level, without a single other vehicle in sight.

All right, then, Jack decided as the minutes slipped by and nothing happened. *Change in plan.* The Edge wasn't out to trap Lieutenant Cue Ball at all. Instead, they were looking for some secret Shamshir base. It was still a trap, Tango Five Zulu was still the bait, only now the Edgemen would wait until they reached their destination to spring it.

He was still holding firmly to that idea fifteen minutes later when the transport settled into a landing.

"Let's go, puppies," Lieutenant Cue Ball said, stepping to the hatchway and waving his gun toward it. "Don't forget about your collars."

Jack was third in line out the door. He glanced first at the sky, to see if the Edge fighters were on their way.

They weren't. Trying hard to keep his hopes up, he lowered his gaze to the area around them.

And with that all of his secret hopes dropped straight into his boots, chewed their way through the soles, and disappeared into the ground beneath him. If this was a secret military base, then he was Draycos's maiden Aunt Matilda.

For starters, the place wasn't even remotely secret. It was completely out in the open, without any large trees, overhanging cliffs, or even camouflage screens to protect it. The Edge training camp on Carrion would have been harder to spot than this place.

It was also very definitely not a military base. The only vehicles in sight were two more Flying Turtles, neither of which looked even slightly armed. A couple of human-style buildings squatted at the edge of the landing area, probably service areas for the transports, probably courtesy of the Shamshir. The rest of the town seemed to be composed entirely of mud huts of various sizes.

"Welcome to Dahtill City," Lieutenant Cue Ball announced as the prisoners looked around them. "Regional capital of this part of Agrist territory, and where this whole thing started."

He smiled, possibly the most unfriendly smile Jack had ever seen. "And for you, puppies," he added, "where it's all going to end."

CHAPTER 18

The mud hut Lieutenant Cue Ball led them to was larger than most of the ones around it, with wide, fan-shaped leaves stuck into its sides at various spots. The doorway was low, and all of them except Rogan had to duck to keep from hitting their heads.

Experimentally, Jack brushed his hand against the outer wall as he went through the doorway. It might look like fresh mud, but it was as hard and unyielding as stone.

A single room took up the entire interior of the hut. There were three aliens seated behind a table in the center: short, pale, hairless beings with round but hollow faces and bright silvery eyes. Agri, Jack decided, though he'd never actually seen any of this particular species up close before. Two of them were wearing the same camouflage military clothing as the Shamshir mercenaries, while the third was dressed in a long white robe with narrow red stripes.

The robe, in Jack's opinion, definitely suited them better. The ones playing soldier looked ridiculous.

"Then tell me what it is this time," the robed Agrist said. His voice was a lot more melodious than Jack would have guessed from the almost skull-like face. "Yet another crushing defeat against the thieves? Another step toward total victory against our oppressors?"

Jack frowned, taking another look. Even given that he didn't know the first thing about reading Agri faces, the robed guy did not seem very happy. In fact, from the tone of the comments, he seemed downright angry. Not exactly the attitude he would have expected.

Unlike Jack, Lieutenant Cue Ball didn't seem surprised by the tone. "I don't blame you for being skeptical, Your Honorest," he said, his voice calm and earnest. "But this time, we have the key."

"These are children," one of the uniformed Agri said harshly. "Human children. Did you think we would not know?"

"Even children can fight, Defense Master," Lieutenant Cue Ball pointed out. "In the hands of capable soldiers like those of the Whinyard's Edge, they can be molded into mighty warriors indeed."

Out of the corner of his eye Jack saw Alison stir. Probably thinking about their ten whole days of training, he decided, and wanting very much to say something sarcastic. But she remained silent.

"But that's not why these particular prisoners are important," Lieutenant Cue Ball went on. "These six are far more valuable than mere warriors. They've been trained in Whinyard's Edge communications and computer access codes. *And* we've also taken their computers intact. Soon we'll be able to break both their real-time tactical data and also learn their long-term plans."

"And this will gain us what?" the robed Agrist asked.

Lieutenant Cue Ball seemed taken aback. "Why, victory, of course, Your Honorest."

"Will it?" His Honorest asked. "Will it really?"

He turned his silvery eyes on Jack. "Will it force the Whinyard's Edge to abandon their attacks on our mine? Will it persuade the Parprins to accept the ruling of the courts that our mine is indeed ours? Will it finally persuade the Trade Association to send a Judge-Paladin to confirm and enforce that ruling?"

Jack felt a funny tingling at the pit of his stomach. Lieutenant Basht had told them that it was the Agri who had jumped the Parprins' mining claims. But according to this Agrist, it was the other way around.

Which was none of his business, of course. He had no particular interest in local politics, or what exactly was going on with a small-time mine that probably no one else in the whole Orion Arm cared about. The only reason he was here was to try to collect information on Djinn-90s, so that he could find out who had attacked Draycos's ships, so that eventually he could get Draycos off his back.

Unfortunately, Draycos wasn't likely to see things quite that simply. Draycos and his K'da warrior ethic were going to be very unhappy if it turned out that they were fighting on the wrong side of this war.

Sure enough, he could feel the dragon moving softly along his skin. That was a sign that usually meant he was uncomfortable or annoyed.

Jack could only hope he would keep his annoyance

to himself long enough for them to get out of this mess.

"The only reason the Parprins are still pushing this is because the Edge is backing them," Lieutenant Cue Ball said. "And the only reason *they're* still on Sunright is that they don't think we can beat them."

"You told us this afternoon's attack in Mer'seb would persuade them to leave," His Honorest said.

"I said it would be the first step," Lieutenant Cue Ball corrected. "What we need now is to bloody them in half a dozen places at once."

He slapped his fingertips at the Edge patch on Jommy's shoulder. "This is our key."

"I do not like this," His Honorest said flatly. "They are children. It is not right to make war against children."

"But it's all right for those same children to make war against us?" Lieutenant Cue Ball demanded, starting to sound impatient. "Come on, think. Use those heads of yours for a change."

"What do you require of us?" the Defense Master asked.

Lieutenant Cue Ball gave a sound that was almost a sniff. "Nothing at all," he said. "We'll get what we need by ourselves. I just thought you'd like to be brought up to speed on what was happening, that's all."

He jerked his head toward the door. The Shamshir soldiers nudged the prisoners, and the whole group turned and went outside again.

"Idiots," one of the soldiers muttered.

"Of course they're idiots," Lieutenant Cue Ball said as he led the way back toward the human-style buildings by the landing area. "All aliens are. Ignore them and concentrate on the job."

"What happens if we don't feel like cooperating?" Alison asked.

Jack winced. It was not a smart thing to say, and he was pretty sure everyone else in the group knew it.

Lieutenant Cue Ball certainly did. "That sounded like a challenge, puppy," he said quietly. "I like challenges. Don't worry, one of you will talk. Maybe you, huh?"

"Lieutenant?" a melodious voice called.

Jack turned to see the second of the uniformed Agri hurrying up behind them. "The Defense Master's compliments. He wishes the human children to be placed in custody under Agrist Protector authority."

"Return the Defense Master's compliments fourfold," Lieutenant Cue Ball said courteously. "And inform him that the prisoners will be delivered to his custody when I'm finished with them."

"The Defense Master specifically said—"

"You will deliver my compliments, and my message," Lieutenant Cue Ball said, turning his back on the alien. "This way, puppies."

He took them into the larger of the two buildings, into a back room that seemed to have been specifically designed to be a jail cell. There were no windows, the door was equipped with two separate locks, and there were a dozen metal rings embedded halfway into the concrete floor.

At Lieutenant Cue Ball's instructions, the soldiers produced handcuffs. Ordering the prisoners to sit, they secured their wrists to the rings. "Right," he said briskly when they were finished. "Someone want to save all of us a lot of time and effort and give me the access codes right now?"

Jack didn't dare look around at the others. He kept his eyes on Lieutenant Cue Ball; and after a moment the man gave a smirk. "Didn't think so," he said. "Fine. We'll do it the hard way.

He looked around the room, and his gaze fell on Jack. "You—Bright Eyes. Let's go."

One of the soldiers unfastened the ring end of Jack's handcuffs, leaving the other end attached to his wrist. Hauling him to his feet, he marched him out of the room. With Lieutenant Cue Ball again in the lead, they took him back outside and into the other building.

The whole procedure seemed to be taking a lot of unnecessary time, Jack thought, especially for people who claimed to be in so much of a hurry. But he'd been through this same routine a few times with various police departments across the Orion Arm. It was all for show: dropping vague threats and then giving the victim time to think and sweat about it.

And the fact that they'd taken Jack out of the room first meant that he wasn't the primary target of the evening's entertainment. Lieutenant Cue Ball hadn't given him nearly enough time to think and sweat, after all.

No, they were probably targeting little Rogan, he decided uncomfortably. Either him or one of the girls.

This second building seemed to be set up more along the lines of the Edge's HQ back on Carrion, with normal offices and hallways and everything. The soldiers took Jack to what looked like a conference room, where he found Tango Five Zulu's fold-top computers laid out neatly around a large oval table. They were plugged in, turned on, and ready to go.

All they were waiting for was the proper access code.

"Okay," Lieutenant Cue Ball said, gesturing to the computers. "Like I said, we can do this easy or we can do it hard. You've got one last chance to be smart."

"Oh, I'm already smart," Jack assured him, watching his face closely. "Problem is, I'm also poor."

Lieutenant Cue Ball's eyes narrowed. "What's that supposed to mean?"

"It means I want to know what's in it for me," Jack said.

One of the other Shamshir snorted loudly. "You get to stay in one piece," he said.

"That's important, all right," Jack agreed, shivering. He needed to play this out, so that he knew how much wiggle room he had here. But at the same time, he definitely didn't want to push these men too far. "But it sounds like you guys are in a hurry. I work faster when I'm inspired."

One of the soldiers took a step forward. "You want inspiration?" he bit out, drawing a long knife from a sheath at his side. "Let me give you some inspiration."

Lieutenant Cue Ball twitched his hand. Reluctantly, Jack thought, the man stepped back. "Okay, I'll play," the lieutenant said. "What do you want?"

"My aunt and uncle indentured me to the Whinyard's Edge," Jack said. "Fifty thousand for two years of slave labor."

"And what, you want us to buy your contract?"

"Hardly," Jack said. "I want cash and a door out of here."

A cynical smile tugged at the corners of Lieutenant Cue Ball's mouth. "I see the Edge is still squeezing a quart of loyalty out of each fresh recruit," he said. "Fine. Cash on the drum for value received. What can you give us?"

"That depends on how much you can pay," Jack countered. "How does a hundred thousand sound?"

"Like you think we're stupid," Lieutenant Cue Ball said darkly. "Or desperate."

"I don't know about the first," Jack said thoughtfully, rubbing at his chin. The loose end of his handcuffs bounced against his chest as he did so. "But on the second, it seems to me that you're pushing up against a deadline here. The Defense Master could send his people around at any time to collect us, you know. I don't think the Agri would like it if they found out you were planning to torture a bunch of human children."

Lieutenant Cue Ball smiled again, a very nasty smile this time. "You think anyone in this room cares a dead frog what the Agri like or don't like?"

Jack frowned. That wasn't the response he'd been expecting. "This is their world," he pointed out cautiously. "They hired *you,* not the other way around."

"I guess maybe you're hard of hearing," Lieutenant Cue Ball said. He wasn't smiling any more. "I'll say it again. I don't care what the Agri like or want, or don't like or don't want. The mine they're sitting on is worth a lot of money. Get the picture?"

Jack looked over at the soldiers standing by the door, feeling the ground sifting like dry sand out from under his position. "So you're not here to defend the Agri at all," he said slowly. "All you want is the mine."

"Catches on quick, don't he?" one of the Shamshir said sarcastically.

"And the only thing that stands in your way," Jack added, "is the Whinyard's Edge."

"Who want the mine just as badly as we do," Lieutenant Cue Ball agreed.

He must have seen something in Jack's face, because he smiled again. "Oh, come now. You weren't thinking noble thoughts about them, were you? Did you really think they were here to help the Parprins take over the mine, collect their fee, and move on? Who do you think they are, Dragonbacks?"

Jack nodded, suddenly feeling very tired. Once, he'd thought he and Draycos were on the right side, helping the Whinyard's Edge defend a Parprin mine from aggressors. A few minutes ago, he'd begun to wonder if it was actually the Agri who were the innocent victims here.

Now, he realized that there was no right side for him to be on. Both armies were out for themselves, fighting solely for a share of the loot. The people who really owned the mine, whichever group it actually was, weren't going to keep their property no matter who won.

Ever since he'd started this scam, Draycos had been talking about how soldiers were the protectors of the weak.

He wondered what the noble K'da poet-warrior would have to say about this.

He didn't have to guess what Uncle Virge would say. *I told you so* pretty well covered that one.

"Yes," he said. "I understand."

He took a deep breath. Draycos had stopped his frustrated movements, he noticed. Perhaps the dragon was offended beyond any reaction at all.

Or else he was preparing for action.

"Good," Lieutenant Cue Ball said. "Don't look so shocked. This is how the universe operates. Get used to it." He folded his arms across his chest. "Here's the offer. Twenty-five thousand, in cash, and a ticket off this mudball for everything in those computers. *If* you can deliver it in one hour."

Jack sighed. Maybe Uncle Virge was right, after all. Maybe looking out for yourself was all you could expect to do in this life. Trying to do anything else was inviting a whole water buffalo stampede to charge right down on top of you.

And at the moment, looking out for himself meant getting out of here. Draycos would understand. In fact, Draycos was probably tugging at the leash to get away from this soggy mess himself.

Anyway, the whole only reason they'd come here in the first place was to track down those Djinn-90s. Twenty-five thousand in Shamshir cash would give them whole new ways to continue that search. That ought to calm the dragon's conscience.

He hoped.

"Deal," he said, stepping to the nearest computer and

sitting down on the chair in front of it. Briefly, he wondered if Draycos would consider this a betrayal of his soldier's oath. But there was nothing he could do except hope the dragon understood. Taking a deep breath, he keyed in the main access code they'd been taught.

Nothing happened.

CHAPTER 19

A quiet alarm bell began jingling in the back of Jack's brain. He tried the access code again. Still nothing.

There were three other codes they'd been taught. He tried each of them in turn, typing slowly and carefully to make sure he wasn't making any mistakes.

None of the codes did anything at all.

The soldiers gathered by the door were beginning to mutter among themselves. Feeling sweat gathering on his forehead, Jack moved over one seat to the next computer in line and tried again. He tried everything again. Still nothing worked.

Lieutenant Cue Ball had started out standing behind Jack, looking over his shoulder. Now, he was crowding so closely against him that Jack could feel him breathing. "What's the matter, Bright Eyes?" he rumbled softly. "Twenty-five thousand suddenly not good enough for you?"

"I don't know what's wrong," Jack protested. "These are the codes they taught us. They worked fine back on Carrion."

"Did they, now," Lieutenant Cue Ball said.

Swallowing hard, Jack attacked the computer one last time. He might as well have saved himself the trouble. "Let me try one more," he offered, starting to get up from his chair.

A big hand landed on his shoulder and shoved him back down into his seat. "Save it," Lieutenant Cue Ball snarled. "You've wasted enough of my time already."

The pressure on Jack's shoulder shifted to a grip under his arm, and he was hauled bodily out of the chair. "Panto, Crick—put him on ice," the lieutenant ordered, giving Jack a rough shove toward the soldiers at the door. "Number Two storeroom. Then go get the Oriental girl. Maybe she'll be more cooperative."

The Number Two storeroom was the mud hut on the far side of the other human-designed building. It was small, no bigger than the *Essenay*'s cargo hold, with a bare dirt floor. Metal shelves stacked with boxes filled most of the floor space, leaving only a few square feet open in the middle. Panto and Crick sat him down in the middle of the open area and attached his handcuff to one of the lower shelf supports. Then they left, turning off the overhead light and closing the door behind them.

Jack sighed, rubbing his eyes tiredly with his free hand. Like the prison cell they'd started out in, this storeroom had no windows, and it was pitch black. "Well," he said aloud. "Here we are."

"Yes," Draycos murmured from his right shoulder. "Can you press up beside these boxes?"

"Yeah, hang on," Jack said, getting up into as high a crouch as he could with his hand chained to the shelf that way. Turning around, he pressed his back against the row of boxes. In their two-dimensional form, K'da had a trick that let them see right through solid objects—though Draycos insisted on saying he was seeing "over" them—provided the walls were thin enough. "How's that?"

There was a sliding sensation on his back as Draycos moved into position. "Anything useful in there?" he asked.

The dragon shifted again, paused, shifted again. Examining all the boxes within reach, probably. There was one final movement, and Jack felt the dragon's head slide back around to rest on his right shoulder. "There is nothing useful to us," he reported. "Two of the boxes contain grenades, while the third contains ammunition. There is nothing that will assist us in a quiet escape."

"Might be helpful in a noisy one, though," Jack pointed out.

"We do not wish a noisy escape, Jack," Draycos said.

"Personally, I don't care what flavor escape we get," Jack grumbled. "You got any ideas?"

"Perhaps," Draycos said. A bit of weight came onto Jack's wrist near the handcuff. "Tell me, what did you do to the computers?"

Jack shook his head. "Not a thing. The codes just didn't work."

"How can that be?"

"Only two possibilities I can think of," Jack said. "Either some idiot got the computers mixed up, or else someone went in and changed all the codes."

Draycos was silent a moment. "Let us follow the chain of reason," he suggested. "Your squad used the computers on the voyage to this world."

"Right," Jack said. "And they were fine during the whole trip."

"They were then transported across the town of Mer'seb to the headquarters building," Draycos went on. "From there they were loaded aboard the Lynx and brought to the outpost at Kilo Seven."

"So if they were switched, it had to have been done in Mer'seb," Jack concluded. "And if they were reprogrammed . . ."

He trailed off. "You have a thought?" Draycos prompted.

"I was just thinking," Jack said slowly. "During the trip to Kilo Seven, they were stacked back in the storage compartment with the rest of the baggage. Anyone could have gone back there and fiddled with them."

"How difficult would it be to alter the codes?"

"I don't know," Jack said. "Uncle Virgil always handled any code-switching we had to do. But I suppose if you'd set up a program card in advance, it could be done pretty quickly."

He tried to reach up to scratch his cheek. The hand came up short as it reached the end of the handcuff chain. "In fact, I'll bet it could even have been done at Kilo Seven while the rest of the squad was getting things set up," he added, examining the restraints with his fingertips. The lock pressed up against the underside of his wrist felt like a standard mechanical handcuff lock. With a proper lockpick, he should be able to open it.

Trouble was, he didn't have a proper lockpick with him. Still, maybe he could find something on the floor; a sliver of metal or something else he could bend into the proper shape. With his free hand, he began feeling carefully around the packed dirt beneath the shelves.

"Alison Kayna," Draycos said suddenly.

Jack's fingers paused in their search. "What about her?"

"She was moving around aboard the Lynx," the dragon reminded him. "She came and spoke with you, in fact."

"Yes, I remember," Jack said, frowning. He'd assumed at the time that she'd just noticed him talking with Sergeant Grisko and decided to be nosy.

But what if that wasn't all of it? What if she'd been back fiddling with the squad's computers? She would have had a clear view of his chat with Grisko from there. "Do you remember if she was in her seat when I was talking to Grisko?"

"I was not able to see in that direction," Draycos said. "At all other times I was watching through the window."

And Jack himself was taking a snooze. The rest of Tango Five Zulu could have thrown a dance party back there for all he knew. "But why would she sabotage the computers?" he asked.

"Why would anyone do so?" Draycos countered.

Jack shrugged. "You got me."

"I do not know either," Draycos said. "However, we suspect that Alison has had previous military training. Her own statement is that she was once with a different group. I do not believe she ever stated which one."

Jack blinked in the darkness. "Are you suggesting she's a spy for the Shamshir?"

"I do not suggest anything in particular," Draycos said. "This situation is not like any I am familiar with."

"Yeah, I don't suppose it is," Jack conceded. "These aren't your kind of soldiers, are they?"

"No, they are not," Draycos said, and Jack could hear the contempt in his voice. "These are little more than thieves in uniforms."

Jack grimaced. "In uniforms, and with high-power rifles."

"The weapons do not matter," Draycos said. "What matters is that they are not true soldiers. I do not believe they will think as warriors do. That gives us an advantage."

"Right." Offhand, Jack couldn't think of any advantages they had at this particular moment, but he wasn't going to argue the point.

For a couple of minutes neither of them spoke. The only sounds were the whistling of the wind against the hardened mud swirls on the outside of their hut and an odd sort of scratching noise Jack couldn't identify. "What are the Shontine like?" he asked suddenly.

"What do you mean?" Draycos asked. "Are you asking about their physical form?"

"No, I saw some of their bodies aboard the *Havenseeker,*" Jack said, shivering at the memory of that trek through debris and death. "I meant what are they like as people. Their personalities, culture—that sort of thing. Are they like you, or are they more like humans?"

Draycos seemed to gather his thoughts. "I do not yet

know your people very well," he said slowly. "You will therefore need to make your own comparisons. The Shontine in general are not violent or aggressive beings. Few indeed are the true warriors born to them, though those few are strongly gifted in their art. Still, even the average Shontin is capable of fighting in his own defense when it becomes necessary to do so."

"But only as a last resort?"

"Mostly," Draycos agreed. "The majority of them prefer to contemplate and appreciate the various forms of their arts, or to create beautiful and useful things with their hands, or to work the soil and bring forth food."

"Sounds like something you'd find on one of the Orion Arm's more backwater worlds," Jack commented.

"I am sure some of your people would consider them primitive and naïve," Draycos said, a little stiffly. "Others would recognize their strength of character and purpose as signs of highly advanced beings. Until the Valahgua began their war against us, their greatest heroes were those who throughout history had stood for what was right amid opposition, even to the point of death."

He moved restlessly against Jack's skin. "Now, sadly, their warriors have become the most esteemed among them. I can only hope they will be able to regain the culture and dignity of their race once they are safely here."

"And I suppose when they are that you'll—?" Jack broke off, suddenly embarrassed at what he'd been about to ask.

But Draycos had caught it anyway. "Do you ask if I will be returning to one of them if we should succeed in our task?"

"Don't get me wrong," Jack said quickly. Too quickly, probably. Uncle Virgil had always said that he talked too fast when he was nervous. "I mean, this arrangement is only supposed to be until they get here. And that's fine with me."

"I will not leave until you wish for me to do so," Draycos said quietly. "I promise you that."

"Yeah," Jack said tartly, blinking back sudden moisture in his eyes. "But no one's exactly sent you an engraved invitation to the royal banquet, either. Uncle Virge and I were doing fine before you showed up, and we'll do fine after you leave."

He leaned back stiffly, wincing as his head bumped against the cold metal of the shelves behind him. "Assuming we ever get out of here," he got himself back on track, wishing he'd never brought up the subject of Draycos's future in the first place. The dragon was a temporary associate. Nothing more. "What does a good poet-warrior do in a situation like this?"

"He does his duty, of course," Draycos said. "The duty of all prisoners of war is to escape."

Jack sighed. "One small problem with that," he said. He snapped his wrist out again to rattle the handcuff chain in reminder.

Only this time the chain didn't rattle. At his first tug it clinked once—

And with a soft thud, the chain snapped off at the cuff around his wrist and dropped in a heap onto the dirt floor.

Jack jerked in surprise, grabbing reflexively at the handcuff around his wrist. Or rather, the ordinary bracelet the cuff had suddenly become. "What in—?"

He broke off, his mouth snapping firmly closed. Of course. The dragon's claws. The claws that he'd once seen scratch a K'da letter into the end of a metal cylinder.

Only this time, the dragon hadn't just scratched. This time, so quietly and stealthily that Jack hadn't even noticed, Draycos had cut his way straight through the handcuff chain.

"You were saying there was a problem?" Draycos said blandly.

Jack glared down at his chest in the darkness. It was impossible to tell, but he could swear the other was laughing at him. "Funny dragon," he growled. "Okay, you're so smart. Now what?"

"As I said, our duty is to escape," Draycos said. Sliding up along Jack's skin to his neck, he popped the control collar free. "But our duty is also to our comrades. We must assist in their release."

"Hold on a second," Jack warned, shivering with relief as he dropped the collar onto the floor and pushed it as far away from him as he could. "If you're suggesting we take on Lieutenant Cue Ball and his troops all by ourselves, you've got a serious argument coming."

"I do not suggest that at all," Draycos assured him. "Our chances for success will be much higher if we leave this place and summon help."

"Now you're talking," Jack said, pushing himself to his feet and brushing the dirt off his hands. "Any idea how we manage that without someone objecting?"

"We begin by opening the door," Draycos said. "Quietly, of course."

"Thanks," Jack said dryly, finding the door handle and easing it open a crack. When it came to sneaking, at least, the noble K'da warrior and the lowly human thief were thinking alike.

Everything seemed quiet outside. Jack stood without moving for a moment, listening to the sounds of the night and watching all the shadows he could see from his angle. Most of the faint background noise seemed to be coming from the Agrist huts in the distance behind them, with nothing closer. Nothing moved, either, at least nothing that he could see. "Looks clear," he murmured. "We going for the Flying Turtles?"

"Would you rather walk?"

Jack rolled his eyes. Draycos was in rare form tonight. Very pleased with himself over the handcuffs, no doubt. "No, let's travel in style, shall we?" he said. "You want to watch our backs?"

A weight formed on his shoulders in response, his jacket pulling tight against his throat as Draycos's head rose up from his shoulder, facing backwards. "Ready."

"Okay." Bracing himself, Jack pulled the door all the way open and stepped into the doorway. He paused there for a moment, watching and listening some more. Still nothing. Closing the door behind him, he slipped out into the night.

CHAPTER 20

He had just reached the first human building, the one where the rest of Tango Five Zulu were handcuffed to the floor, when a slab of light suddenly cut through the darkness ahead.

He dropped into a crouch at the corner, pressing himself against the building. The light, he saw, was coming from the doorway of the second human building. As he watched, two Shamshir soldiers came striding out, supporting a staggering Li between them.

Jack felt his muscles tense. If they took her to the same hut they'd just locked him into, the mustard was about to hit the wiener, big time.

But no. They turned the other direction, their backs to him, and headed toward another row of the small mud huts on the other side of the building.

There was a soft hiss in his ear. "Easy," Jack soothed. "They're not coming this way."

"She has been tortured," Draycos murmured back. There was an edge of barely controlled fury in his voice. "Can you not see that?"

Jack frowned, studying Li's back as she stumbled along. "No, I don't think so," he said. "I remember her looking like she was in shock earlier. I think she's still just not clicking on all chips."

"She does not look right," Draycos insisted. "How can you be certain?"

"Trust me," Jack assured him. "I've seen people scared out of their braincases before."

He nodded toward Li and her escorts. "Besides, look where they're taking her. They're putting her in isolation, same as they did me. That proves she wasn't tortured."

"I do not understand."

Jack sighed. "They're trying to get one of us to break. Right? So they want the ones who are left to be as scared as possible. If they'd really tortured Li, they'd put her back in with the others instead of off by herself."

"Why?"

"So everyone could see firsthand all the gory details," Jack said. "The more scared they are when their turns come, the more likely they'll be to give Lieutenant Cue Ball what he wants."

Draycos's tongue flicked out restlessly. "They put you by yourselves so as to frighten the others?"

"You got it," Jack said. "See, when people keep getting taken away and no one comes back, the ones who are left start wondering what's happened to them. Sometimes that's a whole lot scarier than anything they could dream up on their own."

Draycos was silent a moment. "It is barbaric."

"I suppose," Jack admitted. "But it's better than beating

the sand out of someone. Don't your people ever use psychological warfare?"

"I do not know that term," Draycos said stiffly. "But if it is like this, I am certain we do not."

"Figures," Jack murmured. Sometimes the K'da were too noble for their own good.

The two Shamshir emerged from the hut, minus Li, and turned purposefully toward the building Jack was crouched beside. Going to collect the next contestant in Lieutenant Cue Ball's little game, no doubt. "Keep quiet," he warned Draycos, easing back from the corner out of their sight. "And get ready."

The soldiers reached the door and disappeared inside.

And the second they were out of sight, Jack sprinted for the Flying Turtle they'd been brought here in.

He had estimated he would have about a minute to pop the hatchway and get inside before the soldiers reappeared. As it turned out, the hatchway wasn't locked, and he made it with a good twenty seconds to spare. He was already in the cockpit, studying the control board, when the soldiers came back outside.

With Alison Kayna striding along between them.

"They have taken Alison," Draycos murmured, his head rising from Jack's shoulder for a better look.

"Yeah, I saw," Jack grunted, still sorting out the board. This thing wasn't going to fly much like the *Essenay,* but the controls were similar enough. "Was there something you wanted me to do about it?"

"I was merely observing," Draycos said mildly. "She is not being treated as a fellow Shamshir soldier."

Jack looked up again. The dragon was right. As far as he could tell, she was being marched along the same way he had been earlier, like any other prisoner Lieutenant Cue Ball was hoping to squeeze for information. "Okay, so maybe it isn't the Shamshir she's working for," he conceded. "Maybe it's some other group. Maybe she scrambled the computer codes so that she could be the only one who could pull out the data for them."

"Why?"

"How should I know?" Jack growled. "Maybe she was hired to get in good with the Shamshir. Maybe she was hired to chase the Whinyard's Edge off Sunright. Maybe she just wants to make a cash deal, like I tried to."

Alison and the soldiers disappeared into the building. "And right now, I don't much care," Jack added, keying for startup. "All I want is to get out of here."

The weight on his shoulder shifted as Draycos looked around the cockpit. "Will there not be a recognition code required to start the engines?"

"Probably." Jack gestured to the board. "Conveniently for us, the pilot left this one on standby. I was hoping he had."

Draycos cocked his head. "Careless of him."

"Agreed," Jack said. "But like you said, these guys aren't really soldiers."

He eased in the lifters, and the Flying Turtle rose gently into the sky. "Keep your claws crossed," he warned. "If anyone's going to object, now's the time they're going to do it."

But no one challenged them as they headed off into the night. No one challenged, or signaled, or even seemed to notice. Jack kept the transport close to the ground, putting distance between them and Dahtill City as quickly as he dared, wondering how in the world it was they were getting away so easily.

"It would seem that proper military procedure does not exist here," Draycos commented. "Perhaps the Agri have not allowed their city to be turned into a base for the Shamshir."

"Maybe," Jack said. "Or maybe it's simpler. If this is where the mine is that everybody wants, neither side will want to have any serious fighting nearby."

"Perhaps." Draycos's head rose up higher, his snout pointing past Jack's nose to the left. "Could that be the mine?"

Jack looked that direction. A mile or so past the edge of the city were three dim structures. The center one was much taller than the others, clearly built to house the kind of crane and digging equipment necessary for a deep-ground mine shaft. The other two buildings seemed to be support structures, probably containing supplies and extra equipment. There were only a few lights in evidence, just enough to keep aircraft from running into them. Apparently, the Agri weren't working a night shift.

"Probably," he confirmed. "I seem to remember that daublite is usually deep enough that you have to sink a pretty long shaft to get anywhere near it."

"That sounds expensive."

"Expensive and time-consuming both," Jack agreed.

"The Agri have probably been at this project for years. Maybe even generations."

"Only to then have others try to steal it away from them," Draycos said, sounding disgusted. "Those structures are built over vertical shafts, then?"

"Just the one in the middle," Jack said. "It looks like the pictures I've seen of deep mines."

"A delicate operation," Draycos murmured. "Easily destroyed by accident, or by falling debris collapsing the shaft. I can understand why they do not wish battles nearby."

His head swiveled back toward the view ahead. "This is not the direction to Mer'seb," he said. "From Dahtill City we must turn southwest."

"Right," Jack agreed. "*If* we were heading for Mer'seb. But we're not. We're going back to Kilo Seven."

The dragon's head pulled far enough away from Jack's skin that he could peer at his face. "Is that wise?"

Jack snorted. "In my occasionally humble opinion, 'wise' hasn't been part of the equation since we started this whole job," he said. "But yes, I think it'll get us what we want."

"Explain it to me."

And convince him that Jack was acting like a properly noble K'da warrior? Probably. "First off, the only things the Shamshir took were our squad's own computers," Jack said. "That means all the rest of the Edge stuff is still there. Computers *and* comm equipment. Alison, or whoever, couldn't possibly have sabotaged all of it."

"Then your codes will still allow you access."

"Right," Jack nodded. "So the first thing we'll do is call Mer'seb and whistle up a rescue team. After that, we'll tap into their mainframe and try to pull up the Djinn-90 information that was the reason we came here in the first place."

"You will do that directly?" Draycos asked. "I thought your plan was to use the *Essenay's* equipment and thereby protect yourself from discovery."

"It was," Jack said. "Problem is, the *Essenay* is way to the south somewhere right now."

"Can you not summon it with your comm clip?"

Jack shook his head. "If Uncle Virge is still waiting at November Six, he's way out of comm clip range."

"What about the transmitter in this vehicle? It is more powerful than your comm clip. Could you not tune it to the correct frequency?"

"Sure, but then the conversation wouldn't be encrypted," Jack pointed out. "That means anyone and his toy poodle Mitsy would be able to listen in."

"Perhaps we can use another form of coding," Draycos suggested.

"I don't know how," Jack said. "But it doesn't really matter. I wanted to do a gentle tap into their records so that I could then do a quiet sneak away. But with the Shamshir raid, there's no chance of a quiet sneak anyway. I might as well just bulldoze my way into their mainframe, pull the records, and make a run for it."

"With the *Essenay* still at November Six?"

"Right, but we've got this now," Jack reminded him,

tapping the edge of the control panel. "If we're quick, we should be able to get ourselves down to Uncle Virge before the balloon goes up."

Draycos digested all that. "And you believe you will be able to locate the Kilo Seven outpost?"

"Piece of Boston cream pie." Jack pointed to one of the displays on the board. "Along with not shutting down the transport, the pilot also didn't bother to erase the course memory."

"I see," Draycos murmured. "Convenient."

"And sloppy," Jack said. "But then, they're not real soldiers, are they?"

It had taken Lieutenant Cue Ball fifteen minutes to get them from Kilo Seven to Dahtill City. Ten minutes into the return flight, just as Jack was thinking about cutting their altitude a little, the comm suddenly twittered. "About time," he muttered. "Draycos, how are you at imitating voices?"

"Not very good, I'm afraid," the dragon said.

"Me, neither," Jack said, reaching for the transmission switch. "But maybe I can buy us at least a little more time."

He keyed on the microphone. "Yeah, what do you want?" he demanded in the best imitation of Lieutenant Cue Ball's voice he could manage.

But it wasn't, as he'd expected, some Shamshir flunky wanting to know who had borrowed their transport. "Flying Turtle 505, identify yourself," came an all-too-familiar voice.

Draycos's ears went straight up. "It is Sergeant Grisko," he whispered in Jack's ear.

Jack nodded, feeling suddenly limp with relief. The good guys had finally arrived.

Or at least, the side that wasn't going to be shooting at him had arrived. There were no actual good guys anywhere in this game. "Sir, this is Private Montana," he said, switching back to his normal voice. "Squad Tango Five Zulu. Our group was captured by the Shamshir. I've just escaped."

"Really," Grisko said. "Congratulations."

"Thank you, sir," Jack said. "But they've still got the others. We have to get them out."

"Of course," Grisko said. "Come on in and we'll set something up. You can fly that thing all right?"

"Reasonably well, yes, sir."

"And you're all strapped in?"

"Yes, sir," Jack said, frowning at the speaker. That was a strange question. Come to think of it, Grisko's whole voice was sounding strange. "Shall I put down where our Lynx landed earlier?"

"Sounds good," Grisko said. "Keep 'er steady, and come on in."

The speaker clicked off. "Okay," Jack said, shutting off the comm at his end. "We're set."

"I do not think so," Draycos said, his voice as strange as Grisko's. "Are there emergency escape devices aboard this aircraft?"

Jack frowned. "What in the world—?"

"Do not argue," Draycos snapped, shooting out of Jack's collar to land on the deck behind him. Suddenly the dragon seemed charged with energy and nervous tension.

"We must leave this vehicle at once. Are there escape devices aboard?"

"I can check," Jack said, the urgency in the dragon's voice silencing all questions. "Can you fly this thing?"

"Yes," Draycos said, moving aside to let Jack out of the pilot's seat. "Go. Quickly."

There was a tall storage cabinet built into the wall beside the exit hatchway. Jack started toward it, then changed his mind and instead got down on his knees beside the nearest row of seats.

His second hunch turned out to be right. Strapped beneath each seat was the orange-striped plastic bag of a drop-pack. "Got it," he reported, pulling one free.

"How high must we be to use it?" Draycos asked. He was, Jack saw, curled partially on his side in the pilot's seat, his paws on the transport's controls.

"As high or as low as you want," Jack told him. "It's not like a parachute or hang glider where you need altitude for it to work."

"Then prepare yourself and wait by the door."

"Right," Jack said, ripping open the package tab and heading aft. The drop-pack was similar to the ones he and Uncle Virgil had used once in a midnight skulk onto the roof of a high-rise bank, except that this one had the typical drabness of military surplus. By the time he reached the hatchway, he had it on. "Ready," he called.

"Stand prepared to open the hatchway," Draycos ordered. "When I come to you, we will jump."

Jack took a deep breath, checking all the drop-pack's

straps one final time. The scariest part was that he still didn't know what had spooked the dragon so badly. But anything that worried a poet-warrior of the K'da was definitely something he wanted to be worried about, too.

His eyes fell on the cabinet beside the hatchway. On impulse, he pulled it open.

Originally, he'd thought to find the drop-packs in there. What he found instead was actually more reasonable considering the Flying Turtle's owners.

The cabinet was a weapons locker. The entire top half was filled with the sort of small machine guns Lieutenant Cue Ball and his men had been carrying, with the middle part taken up by shelves full of ammo clips for the guns. At the bottom, looking almost like an afterthought, was a rack holding six slapsticks.

Jack hesitated. The heavier weapons were tempting, but only for a second. Machine guns were mid-range weapons, which was good; but they were also lethal and very noisy, neither of which was what he wanted right now. The slapsticks, on the other hand, were dead quiet and did nothing but knock out your target with an electric shock.

Of course, you also had to get close enough to physically touch him. But you couldn't have everything. Pulling out one of the slapsticks, he made sure it was fully charged, checked to see that the safety catch was on, then stuck it in his belt.

"Prepare," Draycos called.

"Ready," Jack called back, getting a grip on the drop-pack rip cord with one hand and resting the other on the hatchway release pad.

And suddenly, in a flash of golden scales, Draycos spun around and dived out of the pilot's chair. Hitting the top of one of the rows of seats, he shoved off it and bounded toward the hatch.

Jack was ready. He slapped the release; and as the sudden hurricane of wind tore at his hair and clothes he stretched his hand out toward Draycos.

The outstretched forepaws struck his palm and the dragon melted up his sleeve. Pulling the rip cord, Jack pushed off backwards into the night.

The wind grabbed him, and for a horribly tangled second it threw him around, turning him upside down and twice slapping him in the face. It was like being thrown into a raging river made up of air instead of water.

Then the tiny thrusters built into the drop-pack kicked into action. They turned him upright, slowing both his descent and his forward motion. The wind faded, one last set of tree branches grabbed at his sleeve as he passed, and then his feet slapped more or less gently into the crunchy mat of leaves.

"Whew!" he puffed, regaining his balance and looking around. They had landed in a reasonably clear area on a small rise, giving him a good view forward.

There, fading into the distance, he could see their transport. It was still skimming cheerfully away into the night, with no hint of mechanical trouble that he could see.

He shook his head, wondering how many miles they were now going to have to walk. "I don't suppose you happen to know where we are?" he asked.

And then, before Draycos could answer, there was a flicker of light in the distance. Something dark and half-seen seemed to curve up from the forest.

And with a brilliant flash, it exploded against the underside of the Flying Turtle.

CHAPTER 21

The air went out of Jack as if he'd been kicked in the stomach. "Wha—?" he gasped, staring in disbelief at the fireball still hugging the underside of the transport. No—it was impossible.

But even as he watched, even as his mind tried to convince itself that he wasn't seeing what he was seeing, a second object rose from the forest, and a second explosion blasted at the transport's underside.

"That attack was meant for us," Draycos said, his voice low and grim as his head rose from Jack's shoulder. "I see your military vehicles are well equipped with ventral armor."

The words seemed to bounce around Jack's brain like angry hornets trying to get through a window. "What are you talking about?" he heard himself say.

"Ventral armor," Draycos repeated. "Protection for the underside of the craft. Designed to protect the troops being carried."

Jack tore his eyes away from the Flying Turtle, wavering but still holding together, and stared at the dragon's face. "Are you insane?" he demanded. "Someone just tried to kill us, and you're talking equipment specs?"

"Be calm, Jack," Draycos advised. With a surge of weight

and pressure, he leaped out of Jack's collar and landed on the ground in front of him. "I do not believe they intended to kill you. I believe they meant only to disable the craft, so that you could be taken prisoner."

A distant clattering sound wafted toward them on the night air, like a bunch of spoons that had been dropped into a sausage grinder. Jack looked over, to find that the Flying Turtle had finally given up and disappeared into the trees.

He didn't have any trouble seeing where it had landed, though. The reddish glow of the fire from its burning fuel tanks was plainly visible.

"I don't believe this," he muttered. "They shot down one of their own transports just so they could grab me again? That's crazy. They already know I can't get them into our computers."

Draycos twisted his long neck. "You misunderstand, Jack," he said darkly. "It was not the Shamshir who did this."

Jack frowned at him. "You can't be serious."

"I am very serious," Draycos assured him. "It was the Whinyard's Edge who shot down the transport."

"But that doesn't make sense," Jack protested. "I was already on my way to meet them. Why shoot at me?"

"I do not know," Draycos said. "But remember: Sergeant Grisko asked if you were strapped in. And he instructed you to keep your course steady."

"That was just a figure of speech," Jack muttered. But even as he argued, he knew down deep that he was batting at flies here. He'd spent over two weeks with Grisko, and never in that time had he heard the man utter a single word of concern for anyone's safety. Plus, there'd been that odd tone in his voice just before he signed off.

And he and Uncle Virgil had been betrayed too many times over the years for him not to know what it felt like to be stabbed in the back.

"But why?" he asked. "What did I ever do to him?"

"That is what we must find out," Draycos declared.

The dragon had been gazing out at the sky as if trying to find constellations in the unfamiliar star patterns. Now, he looked back at Jack and flipped his tail up in front of the boy's face. "The sky is clear of watchers. Take hold."

"Wait a second," Jack protested even as he got a grip on the end of the dragon's tail. "Where are we going?"

Draycos lifted a forepaw. "The transport is there," he said, pointing a forepaw toward the glow. "The Kilo Seven outpost is there," he went on, shifting his forepaw about forty-five degrees to the right. "Between them is the sentry cage you occupied earlier this evening. I wish to intercept them near there."

"Yeah, well, just wait a second," Jack said cautiously. This whole thing had to be some kind of huge misunderstanding. The last thing he wanted was for a gung ho K'da warrior to go off the high dive into the revenge pool. "They didn't kill anyone. Right? No hospital, no foul."

Draycos tossed his head. "You misunderstand, Jack," he said. "I do not seek vengeance, but information."

"And how exactly do you expect to get it?"

"We shall see," Draycos said. "Now. Let us go."

. . .

Earlier that night—was it still just the same night?—Jack had hurried back from the sentry cage to the outpost. At the time, he would have sworn that that was as fast as it was possible for him to travel through a dark forest without breaking a leg or clotheslining himself on a low-hanging branch.

He'd been wrong. He'd been very wrong.

They raced through the forest. Not a quick walk, not a cautious jog, but a flat-out run. Draycos was in a hurry; and a K'da warrior in a hurry was a sight to behold.

And the most astonishing part of it was that Jack never even so much as twisted an ankle.

He never did figure that one out. Yes, he knew that Draycos had a different kind of eyesight than humans, which clearly included better night vision along with the rest of the package. And yes, the dragon also had training and experience in moving around different types of terrain.

But that only explained how Draycos kept from hurting himself. How he managed to also keep Jack's feet from finding any dips or tree roots along the way remained a mystery.

For the first ten minutes or so Draycos kept the pace as fast as Jack could manage, stopping every couple of hundred yards for a quick breather. Or at least, that was what Jack first thought the rest stops were for. It was only after the third one that he realized the dragon wasn't so much calling a time-out as he was pausing to listen for signs of their opponents.

It was at the ninth rest stop that those sounds began to be

heard, at least by K'da ears. From that point on, they walked quietly instead of running.

There was no conversation. There was no need for any. Jack might not have K'da military training, but he knew all about sneaking through hostile territory trying not to be noticed.

They had gone another ten minutes, and Jack had just about gotten his breath back from that mad dash, when Draycos abruptly came to a halt. Jack froze in place beside him, listening hard.

For a moment there was nothing. Then, from somewhere ahead, he heard it: a quiet voice, two more acknowledging voices, and then a faint crackle of leaves. Slowly, the crunching sounds moved off.

"Careful," he whispered into Draycos's ear as the sounds faded away. "They might have left a guard behind."

The dragon's tongue flicked out twice, tasting the air. "No," he whispered back. "All three have gone ahead. But others are moving up behind them."

Jack swallowed. Terrific. "What now?"

"We need information," Draycos said. "We must therefore set a trap. You spoke earlier of electronic detectors?"

Abruptly, belatedly, Jack remembered the slapstick at his side. "Oh, geez," he breathed, snatching it out of his belt like he'd suddenly found a snake riding his hip. "I wasn't even thinking."

"Calm yourself," Draycos assured him. "I allowed you to bring it because it may now be useful. Come."

He headed off at an angle. Gripping the slapstick in one hand and Draycos's tail in the other, Jack followed.

The dragon led him in a curving path, stopping at last beside a small tree with slender, multiple trunks poking out from a twisted root system. "Here," he said. "You may put the weapon down."

Jack obeyed. As he did so, something set between two of the thin trunks caught his eye. It was a small plastic object, shaped like a curved cone with a flat piece of glass or plastic on the side facing away from him. A thin metal rod connected it to one of the trunks, and he could see a double cable attached to the cone's pointy end hanging down to the ground.

And suddenly he realized what it was. "That's one of the Argus eyes!"

"Yes," Draycos agreed. "Do not worry. We have come up behind it." He reached out a claw and deftly sliced one of the two cables near where it went into the cone. "At any rate, they cannot see from it now."

"Yes, but—" With an effort, Jack choked back his protest. If anyone had been looking at the monitor when Draycos cut the cable, he might just as well have sent up a flare announcing where they were. "Fine. What now?"

The dragon's jaws opened slightly. "Now," he said, "we find you a tree."

Jack blinked. "A tree?"

"One which will hide you, but which they will not expect you can climb," Draycos continued, looking around. "One which therefore they will not think to examine. Ah—there. Come."

He headed off toward a smooth-sided tree that showed a hint of a bush-like branch structure beginning about fifty feet up. Rather like a giant dandelion, Jack thought as they approached. "Hold tightly," Draycos ordered, leaping a few feet up onto the side of the tree and again wagging his tail into Jack's face.

Swallowing hard, Jack got a firm grip on the tail. Without seeming to even notice the extra weight, Draycos started to climb.

A minute later they had reached the branches. "This should conceal you well," Draycos decided, pushing aside one of the leafy branches with his forepaw.

"Yeah," Jack agreed. Actually, with the way the branches spread out in layers from the trunk, each layer perhaps three feet higher up on the trunk than the previous one, the setup was like a woody sort of hammock with an overhead canopy. A lot cozier than some of the places he'd hidden out over the years.

Provided, of course, you weren't afraid of heights. "Where are *you* going to be?"

Draycos turned head downward, again gripping the trunk with his claws. "As I said, I will be setting a trap," he said. "Wait here until I return."

He headed down. "Sure," Jack murmured. "Whatever you say."

CHAPTER 22

Jack had been trying his best, Draycos knew. And he'd done a remarkably good job, given his youth and inexperience. Draycos appreciated that well, and once again was reminded that he could travel far and long here in the Orion Arm without finding a better partner.

But for all his effort and willingness, the boy was not a warrior. And to be honest, that meant he couldn't help but be a certain amount of dead weight. Both for that reason, and of course for Jack's own safety, Draycos was glad to have the boy out of the way for the moment.

Now, he thought grimly as he moved down the tree trunk, their opponents would see what a poet-warrior of the K'da could do.

Or to be more precise, they *wouldn't* see it. If all went well, they wouldn't see a thing.

The first advance team was long gone by now, heading downslope toward the wreckage of the transport. But there were at least two more groups within earshot making their way stealthily through the forest. All of them human, Draycos decided as he tasted the air.

He didn't know why the Whinyard's Edge seemed to have

few if any nonhumans among their ranks. But that curious fact would make this particular task easier. After nearly two months with Jack, human physical capabilities were a known quantity to him, and fairly easy to work into his strategy.

He made his way back to where he'd left the Argus sensor and Jack's slapstick. The sensor was fastened solidly into the tree, but a little digging with his claws and he soon had it free. Tucking the sensor and slapstick under his forearms, he headed back in the direction of the Kilo Seven outpost, trailing the sensor's twin cables behind him.

He had to pause three times along the way, curling around himself and freezing to complete motionlessness beneath a convenient bush or thicket, as he ran into more trios of searchers. He studied each group carefully as they passed, trying to decide if they were all mere foot soldiers or whether one of them might be the line commander he was seeking.

In each case, he concluded it was the former. Apparently, the commander was still somewhere in the rear, allowing his men time to neutralize any threats before moving out himself.

For their part, not surprisingly, none of the soldiers took any notice of him, despite whatever sensor equipment and night-vision devices they might be carrying. Intent upon locating a human fugitive, they had no interest in a motionless creature of an unfamiliar type.

Even with the stops, it took only a few minutes for him to reach the sentry cage Jack had been manning earlier that night. No one was visible there, and for a few seconds he studied the area from cover, mentally putting the final touches on his plans. Then, tasting the air once more to confirm that no one was nearby, he set to work.

The first step was to replant the Argus sensor where it would be partially visible from the sentry cage. He found a good spot about fifty feet away to the south, half hidden beneath a bush. He wedged the metal mounting rod into the ground, leaving the sensor itself free to rotate. Then, leaving the slapstick beside it as bait, he began playing out the cable toward the sentry cage.

But not directly toward it. Twenty feet to the east of the tree that marked the cage was another of the puff-top trees like the one where he'd left Jack. Dropping his end of the twin cables near the base, he crossed to the cage and sliced the cables at that end. The two cables, he had already noted, were held only loosely together by a series of connector loops. Gripping the monitor end of both cables in his jaws, he climbed up into the puff-top tree.

Earlier, he had cut the sensor cable where it entered the Argus eye. Now, careful not to let it get hung up, he pulled the sensor cable completely through the connectors, freeing it from the control cable and coiling it up as it came. When the far end finally came free, he had a coil of over two hundred fifty feet.

The other end of the control cable was still connected to the sensor. He gave it a quick examination, confirming that he could operate the mechanical linkage with his claws, then wrapped the end around a branch for safekeeping. Hoisting the coil of sensor cable over his shoulder, he leaped across to the sentry-cage tree, the one the round Argus monitors were attached to. He worked his way around the trunk, then jumped to the next tree over.

He'd noticed this type of tree earlier that evening during his brief search for enemy soldiers. It had two very different types of branches: one of them solid and unyielding, the other equally solid but far more flexible and springy. Choosing one of the second type, he tied one end of his sensor cable to it and threw the rest of the coil back over to the Argus tree.

Leaping back to the Argus tree himself, he got a firm grip on the trunk and began to pull on the cable, bending the springy branch back toward him.

The farther he bent it, naturally, the more resistant it became to being bent any farther. It took every bit of his strength, plus some very fancy claw work, to finally work it all the way into position.

But finally he had it in place. Tying the center of the cable to one of the Argus tree's thickest branches with a quick-release knot, he gathered up the remainder of the coil and leaped back to the puff-top tree on the other side. Climbing up to the third layer of branches, he moved a few feet along one of the thicker limbs to a conveniently placed fork. Looping his end of the cable around it, he returned the coil to his shoulder and jumped back to the Argus tree.

He could hear the sound of footsteps now, several sets of them, coming from the direction of the Kilo Seven outpost. Most were the cautious movements of the patrol soldiers he'd evaded earlier, but one was the slightly noisier tread of a senior officer who had perhaps forgotten proper sneaking technique.

The line commander, it seemed, had finally decided to

join his men in the field. Fortunately, the trap was nearly set.

He climbed down the Argus tree with what remained of his coil, taking care that the cable not get hung up on any of the branches. At the lowest layer of branches—with this type of tree, they were no more than eight feet above the ground—he pulled the cable taut and tied another quick-release knot connecting it to a branch.

That left him perhaps ten feet of loose cable. He tied a slipknot loop in the end, draped it out of sight across two branches, then climbed back to his first quick-release, the one holding the springy branch taut. A gentle pull released it, and there was a soft twanging sound as the rest of the cable took up the tension.

For a moment he crouched there in the upper branches, tracing the cable with his eyes, making sure he'd gotten everything exactly as he'd planned. From the bent springy branch, through the edge of the Argus tree to the puff-top tree. Looped around a third-level branch there, back to the Argus tree, quick-release knot at the lowest branches, the rest in a slipknotted loop.

Perfect.

Leaping once more to the puff-top, he retrieved the control cable and returned one last time to the Argus tree. Moving down the trunk, he set himself on the far side from his approaching opponents, hiding in a thick clump of leaves.

And everything was now ready. Everything, that was, except for the one unknown still in the equation. The question of whether the commander and his men would behave as expected.

There was no way for him to know. No way even for him to guess, really, at least not with any certainty. Human reflexes he understood; human eyesight, too, and hearing and stamina and strength.

But in many ways, human ways of thinking were still foreign to him. Their ways of thinking, and their behavior, and their basic fundamental reactions.

And if he had guessed wrong, all his effort would have been for nothing.

Still, he'd gone this far. He might as well see it through. Besides, Jack surely understood his own species; and hadn't Jack agreed that these people didn't act like true soldiers?

Peering around the side of the trunk, he could see the approaching group as they moved cautiously through the trees toward him. There were five in all: four patrol soldiers plus the one who didn't step as cautiously as his companions.

Like the others, the latter's face was obscured by the half-helmet he was wearing to support his night-vision equipment. From his build, though, Draycos could see that it wasn't Sergeant Grisko.

Pity. After Grisko's part in the betrayal and attack on the transport, he would rather have liked to deal with that one personally.

The group was nearly to the sentry cage now. Keeping his movements small, Draycos dug his claws delicately into the meshed steel lines inside the control cable and gently tugged.

There was no reaction from the Edgemen. Draycos tugged again, this time risking a quick look over at the half-hidden sensor. It was moving, all right, turning slowly back and forth.

Still no response. Draycos tried again, beginning to think unkind thoughts about his opponents' competence. *He* could see the faint reflection glinting from the sensor's face. Why couldn't they?

And then, just as he was wondering whether he should give up the effort, one of the soldiers spotted it. He snapped his arm up, his fingers rapidly tracing out hand signals Grisko had never bothered to teach Jack and his fellow recruits.

The four patrol soldiers responded with all the smooth efficiency of professionals. Without fuss or hesitation, they drifted to both sides as they continued forward, moving to flank whoever it was watching them from beneath the bush.

The fifth man did not join them. Instead, he eased into the sentry cage and stopped, watching nervously from behind the Argus tree.

Draycos felt his jaws crack in an ironic smile. So he and Jack had been right. A true warrior line commander would have gone with his men into danger, taking the same risks they did so that he could issue prompt and reasonable orders if it became necessary.

Instead, this commander was hiding from the danger. Sending his men into the unknown was all right, but he wasn't willing to even get his own scales dusty.

As a warrior, Draycos could feel only contempt for such behavior. But as the man's opponent, he could feel an equally strong satisfaction.

Because in his effort to protect himself, the commander

now stood directly behind the very tree Draycos was cling-ing to.

Exactly where Draycos wanted him.

The control cable had served its purpose. Laying it aside, Draycos got a good grip with his left forepaw on the slip-knotted loop of sensor cable. Beside him was the quick-release knot that held the whole thing in place. Carefully, he eased the tip of his tail into the release loop.

The patrol soldiers were closing on the sensor now. Dray-cos waited; and abruptly, one of them snorted. "Cute," he mur-mured. "It's one of our own Argus eyes, sir. No one there."

"But I saw it moving," one of the others insisted.

"So did I," the first confirmed, hefting his gun as he looked around. "And the slapstick Barkin spotted on the scan is here, too. Probably bait. Like I said, someone's being cute."

"Trace the cable," the commander ordered in a hoarse whisper. "Find him."

"Yes, sir," the first soldier said, moving toward the Argus eye as the others fanned out toward the surrounding trees.

The commander hesitated another moment. Then, cau-tiously, he slipped out from behind the Argus tree. Either get-ting his courage back, or else simply unwilling to get too far away from the protection of his men and their weapons. Cir-cling the trunk, he started toward them.

And in that fraction of a second, as he passed beneath Draycos, the K'da warrior struck.

Releasing his rear claws, he dropped to the same level as the commander's head before grabbing hold of the tree again.

With his right forepaw he slashed the chin strap holding the man's helmet in place, and in the same motion flicked the helmet up and off his head.

Reflexively, the commander grabbed for the helmet as it spun away into the night. Draycos was ready with the loop, dropping it over his head and arms and giving it a quick tug to tighten the slipknot around his ribs. At the same time, he slammed his right paw against the side of the commander's head behind his ear, a spot that experience had showed was a good place to knock out a human without too much risk of serious damage.

And even as the commander sagged unconscious in the loop of cable, Draycos flicked the quick-release with his tail and dropped to the ground.

The quiet of the night was abruptly shattered. As the cable tension was suddenly released, the springy tree branch off to Draycos's right snapped back to its original position. It slapped and scattered all the other branches in its way as it moved, sending a small shower of leaves fluttering to the ground.

The unconscious commander, tied to the other end of the cable, went the other direction. Shooting up and to the left, he disappeared up into the puff-tree's branches.

The soldiers, facing the wrong direction, saw none of it. But they could hear just fine; and as they spun back around they could see the shower of leaves drifting down from the springy tree. "Sir!" one of them snapped.

"He's gone!" someone else barked. "What the—?"

"Over there," the first soldier said, pointing toward the

springy tree with his gun. "Barkin, Schmidt—check it out. Watch for more booby traps. Tomasaki, keep your eyes open. It might be a diversion."

Two of the soldiers ran toward the springy tree, alternately peering up into the branches and watching the ground where they were walking. The other two crouched low where they were, facing opposite directions with their guns held ready.

Keeping to the cover of the underbrush, Draycos crept out of the sentry cage and made a wide circle back toward the puff-top tree. The patrol soldiers knew their business, all right. They'd quickly guessed the style of snare trap he'd just sprung on their commander.

The only trouble was, they were looking for him in the wrong tree.

He reached the puff-top tree about the same time they arrived at their own destination. Putting the trunk between him and the two guards, he started up. If either of the soldiers at the springy tree happened to turn around, he knew, they would spot him easily. But with their attention elsewhere, he wasn't expecting either to do so.

And they didn't. He made it to the safety of the branches while they were still staring uselessly skyward.

The commander was hanging limply out of sight among the leaves, bobbing a little as the springy tree branch across the way waved gently in the breeze. Draycos got him up and lying securely across the branches, then cut the cable.

He climbed a little higher into the tree, coiling the cable as he went. He wasn't really expecting the soldiers to go so far as to climb the springy tree in their search for their missing commander. Still, it was a possibility; and if they did, he didn't want them tracing the cable back here. Moving out onto one of the branches, he lobbed the coil across into the upper part of the Argus tree.

"He's not here," one of the soldiers at the springy tree reported.

"That's impossible," the first soldier insisted. "Check it again."

"I did," the other said. "Twice, visual and IR both. He's not up there."

The first soldier swore. "A diversion, all right. Okay, spread out. Let's find him."

"Right. Better call it in."

"No kidding," the first said sarcastically. "Base, this is Hernandez. We've got a problem."

Listening to the conversation with half an ear, Draycos climbed back down to the unconscious commander. The human was wearing two separate comm clips, he discovered. Even with them turned off, they might be traceable.

Easily dealt with. K'da forelegs were too short for him to throw anything that light very far, but there were other ways. Making sure the comm clips were turned off, he placed them together and wrapped them in the tip of his tail. A quick flip, sling-fashion, and they sailed off into the night.

Using the short length of cable still looped under the commander's arms, Draycos tied the human's wrists and ankles. One of his pockets yielded a headband, while another contained a handkerchief. The handkerchief made an adequate gag; the headband was quite suitable for securing the man's hood down over his eyes.

And now all that was left was to wait for the search to burn itself out and move to another area. Crawling onto the underside of the branches, he found himself some convenient claw-grips directly beneath the commander.

After all, the searchers might eventually think to look up into this tree. And as Jack had pointed out, a K'da heat profile did not look anything like a human's.

An hour, he estimated, and he and Jack would be free to move again. Stretching his muscles once, he settled down to wait.

CHAPTER 23

The commander was awake by the time Jack let go of Draycos's tail and got himself seated more or less securely on the branches facing him. "You sure there isn't anyone else around?" he muttered as Draycos climbed around behind the prisoner.

The dragon shook his head, but remained silent. Jack understood; he didn't want the prisoner to hear his voice. "Okay," he said briskly. "Let's get this over with." Grabbing hold of the cable tying the man's wrists together, he started to pull him up into a sitting position.

The other responded by trying to grab Jack's hand. "Hey, hey, take it easy," Jack warned, yanking his hand back out of reach. "Don't struggle or try anything stupid. You're fifty feet off the ground in a very leaky tree."

The man seemed to see the logic in that. He grunted behind his gag and subsided. "All we want is a little chat," Jack went on, pulling him upright again. This time the other didn't struggle. "A *quiet* little chat," he added. "You try shouting for help and we'll have to shut you up. A fair chance we'll lose your balance in the process. Understand?"

The man grunted again. Jack glanced at Draycos, making

sure the dragon was standing ready but out of the prisoner's sight. Then, reaching over, he pulled off the gag.

"Montana?" the other rumbled, his voice the croak of a man with too dry a mouth. He worked his lips a moment and tried again. "It's Montana, isn't it?" he demanded.

Jack started. He knew that voice. "Colonel Elkor?" he asked, pulling off the headband and lifting the man's hood.

It was Colonel Elkor, all right, glaring at Jack like he was trying to push him out of the tree by sheer willpower. "Well, well," Jack said, filling in time as he tried to get his brain rebooted. He'd expected Sergeant Grisko or maybe Lieutenant Basht to be leading this charge. To have a full colonel show up meant this was bigger than he'd thought.

"You're a pretty big fish to be flopping around in this size pond," he went on. "I guess I never saw you as the great outdoors type."

"I wondered about you," Elkor growled. "So is Kayna working for you? Or is it the other way around?"

He started to turn. Draycos batted him warningly against the side of the head and he seemed to think better of the idea. "I'll bet it's Kayna who's calling the shots," he decided. "Who are you working for? The Shamshir, or someone else?"

"This is my interrogation, thanks all the same," Jack said. "But just for the record, I'm not working for anyone."

Elkor snorted derisively. "Right. You just felt like a midnight stroll one night. And then, what, you needed to use the latrine?"

Jack shook his head. "I already told you. The Shamshir sneaked into the camp and captured us. I escaped and—"

"Don't play dumb," Elkor cut him off harshly. "I'm talking about back on Carrion."

"Oh," Jack said, a little lamely. "That."

"Oh. That," Elkor mimicked. "Basht was pretty sure it was Kayna. But I wondered about you. If we'd had time to really check out your application—"

"Wait a second," Jack said, frowning as he thought back on that failed midnight raid. Was he suggesting that had been *Alison* coming up the stairs? "I'm sorry, but I'm confused here. What does Alison have to do with any of this?"

For the first time Elkor's glare seemed to crack a little. "Are you saying that *wasn't* you in the HQ building?"

Jack hesitated. Common sense, plus years of Uncle Virgil's tirades on the subject, said you never gave away information for free. But he was thoroughly lost here, and he had the odd feeling that Elkor wasn't exactly sitting steady on this stack of blocks either. Maybe it would be worth pooling their information a little.

"I did sneak into the HQ, yes," he told Elkor. "I was looking for some computer data. But I had to run for it when someone headed my direction laying down a sopor gas pattern. I assumed at the time it was a guard."

Elkor snorted again. "Trust me, if it *had* been one of us you would have known it. Sopor gas is for sissies."

"Or for people who don't want anyone knowing they'd been there," Jack pointed out. "So you think that was Alison?"

Elkor regarded him coolly. "So what computer information were you looking for?"

Jack shrugged. "Fine. Have it your way."

He began shaking out the handkerchief he'd taken from around the colonel's mouth. "Even with the gag, I'll bet they'll be able to hear you from down there. Assuming they ever come back to this area to look, of course."

He reached the handkerchief toward Elkor. The other leaned away, then jerked as Draycos caught his head firmly between his forepaws. "Wait a second," he said hastily. "All right, all right. What do you want to know?"

"I want to know what's going on," Jack told him, lowering the handkerchief but keeping it in sight. "You can start by telling me what happened to the rest of the Edgemen at Kilo Seven."

Elkor's lips compressed into a thin line. "We pulled them out," he said grudgingly. "We knew the Shamshir would be raiding the place and didn't want them getting hurt."

"Oh, I see," Jack said. "You didn't care enough about *us* to even warn us, but—"

He broke off, staring at the man. Suddenly, it was all making terrible sense. "You called the Shamshir down on us, didn't you?" he said. "You *let* them capture us."

"One of you was a spy and a traitor," Elkor said. "In the Whinyard's Edge, we know how to deal with traitors."

He smiled unpleasantly, clearly enjoying Jack's discomfort. "Now, now, don't pout," he said, mock-soothingly. "What are you going to do, call foul and run crying home to Mommy? This is the real world, kid. Get used to it."

"What about the others?" Jack asked, ignoring the gibe. "Why didn't you just take Alison and me out and shoot us, if that was what you wanted?"

"Not very sporting to line you up against a wall," Elkor said. "Besides, we didn't just want you dead. We wanted information. We figured that if you were working for the Shamshir, one of you would get a big welcome when they snatched you."

He cocked his head. "Or else one of you would come back and claim to be an escaped hero."

"And if we weren't working for the Shamshir?"

Elkor shrugged. "You were working for *someone*. Might as well let the Shamshir beat it out of you than bother with it ourselves."

Jack hissed between his teeth. "And of course, you couldn't let us take working computer codes to them," he said. "So you made sure you scrambled them before we landed on Sunright."

"After we landed, actually," Elkor said offhandedly. "Not that it matters."

"No, not really," Jack said. "So who's behind all this?"

Elkor frowned. "Who's behind all what?"

"Who's pulling your strings?" Jack amplified. "Who's really after this mine? Is it Cornelius Braxton?"

Elkor snorted. "Don't be ridiculous. You think someone as big as Braxton would even notice an operation this small?"

"Arthur Neverlin, then?" Jack persisted.

"Never heard of him."

"But then—"

"No one pulls our strings, kid," Elkor cut him off coldly. "No one but us. If whoever you're working for is thinking about trying to bulldoze his way into this, you can tell him to forget it. Once we've got hold of that mine, it's going to be ours, period. No one else is going to get a piece of it. You got that?"

"Yeah, I got it," Jack said. So Lieutenant Cue Ball had been right. Neither mercenary group cared a downwind spit about the people they'd been hired to protect. They were in it for the daublite mine, and that was it. "It's so much easier to fight and kill and steal someone else's mine than go dig one yourselves."

"Mines cost money," Elkor countered. "Lives are cheap. Do the math."

"Yeah, well, some lives are apparently cheaper than others," Jack said. "That still doesn't explain why you threw Jommy and the rest of them to the wolves along with Alison and me."

Elkor sniffed. "What's this 'and me' stuff? Kayna was the chief suspect, not you. You were just one of the known contacts."

Jack blinked. "The what?"

"She talked to you, Montana," Elkor said patiently. "Grisko told us. Alone, and at length, out on the shooting range. Do I have to draw you a picture?"

Jack stared at him in disbelief. "Let me get this straight," he said slowly. "Alison has a chat with, say, Rogan Mbusu, maybe about nothing more classified than the lousy food. And suddenly you're just going to throw him away? Just on the off chance that she *might* have passed secret information to him?"

"You make the assumption that any of you were worth

much to begin with," Elkor said. "You ever hear the term 'cannon fodder'?"

Jack swallowed hard. "Yes."

"It's rather out of date, actually," Elkor went on. "No one but a few primitives use real cannon anymore. But the term still applies."

"Kind of an expensive hobby," Jack murmured. "You still have to pay all of our indenture fees."

"You should read the contract more closely sometime," Elkor suggested blandly. "There are all sorts of neat clauses that cover death or capture in a war zone when the subject has failed to properly defend himself. Another good reason to bring you out here instead of dealing with you back on Carrion."

He lifted his eyebrows. "You *did* fail to defend yourselves, didn't you? I hadn't heard any reports of gunfire."

For a long moment Jack just looked at him, wondering what Draycos would say if he reached over and pushed the smug son of a snake out of the tree. Uncle Virgil would have, he suspected. Even Draycos, for all his warrior ethic, was crouched there with his eyes burning like those of an avenging angel. He probably wouldn't lift a single claw to save scum like this.

He took a deep breath. No. He'd never been a killer, or even an avenger. He'd been a thief; and even there he was supposed to be reformed.

And he was probably selling Draycos short anyway. The dragon had gotten that look in his eye before, and he hadn't murdered anyone yet.

"You are a small, petty, pathetic little man," he told Elkor quietly. "You deserve to die. With any justice, it'll be at the hands of your own people."

Elkor's mouth twitched in a lopsided smile. "So you don't even have the guts to kill me, huh? You're no soldier, Montana. You never will be."

"I can live with that," Jack told him. "Incidentally, I *have* lived in the real world, sometimes among people who would have pushed you out of this tree ten minutes ago if you'd done this to them."

Elkor snorted. "If you're hinting that you've got friends, save it," he said. "I don't scare that easily."

"I'm not trying to scare you," Jack said. "And none of them are my friends. I was simply pointing out that none of *them* ever tried to kill the casual acquaintances of people they were mad at. Even *they* had more class than that."

"Did I say I needed your approval?" Elkor asked. "Or even wanted it?"

"Hardly," Jack said, suddenly thoroughly weary of this man. "Fine. We're going. Where are your transports?"

A slight frown creased Elkor's forehead. "Why?"

"Why do you think?" Jack retorted. "So we can get out of here. Don't worry, I'm not going to steal it. All I want is to use the comm."

"And you think I'm going to tell you?"

With a sigh, Jack pulled out the small folding knife from his belt pack. He locked it open and waved it under Elkor's eyes. "That cable you're tied with is pretty tough," he reminded the other. "Even with this, it'll take you quite awhile to cut through it. Would you rather use your teeth?"

Elkor eyed the knife. "They're on the west side of the outpost," he muttered. "In a clearing about two hundred yards due west of the sentry cage on that side. But you'll never make it past the guards."

"We'll take our chances." Reaching up, Jack drove the tip of the knife blade into the tree trunk a couple of feet above Elkor's head. "Help yourself after we're gone," he said, pulling the colonel's hood over his eyes again.

Catching Draycos's eye, he nodded. "Come on, buddy," he said. "Let's go."

They headed down the tree, Draycos climbing down backwards as Jack dangled onto his tail beneath him. They reached the ground without incident and headed off through the woods toward the area where Elkor had said the transports were located. If they weren't there, Jack promised himself darkly, he would make sure to send Draycos back up the tree and get his knife back.

"Then the disturbance outside the training camp was a diversion for Alison's benefit?" Draycos murmured as they slipped through the trees.

Jack blinked, forcing himself back from half-hoped-for scenarios of revenge. "What? Oh. Yeah, I suppose that makes the most sense. I wonder who she's working for."

"We had already decided it was not the Shamshir," Draycos reminded him. "Could it be a different mercenary group?"

Jack frowned. With his own chances of escape weighing

heavily on his mind, the last thing he was interested in right now was Alison Kayna's possible background and friends. Still, it was an intriguing question. "I don't think so," he told the dragon slowly. "With all that's happening here, it would make sense for the Shamshir to send in whoever they had handy to grab some quick information about the Edge's plans for Sunright. But any other merc group ought to be able to take the time to find an adult to use as a spy instead of a kid."

Draycos seemed to digest that. "Then who *is* she working for? Were we wrong about her connection to the Shamshir?"

"I don't know," Jack said as a sudden and very unpleasant thought sent a creepy sensation tingling across the back of his neck. "You don't suppose she might be working for Neverlin, do you?"

"I thought we decided he was too busy hiding from Braxton to bother us."

"*You* decided that," Jack countered. "*I* never did."

The dragon twitched his tail. "I do not believe Neverlin could have moved this quickly," he said firmly. "And how could he have known we would be joining this particular mercenary group? Alison was clearly already signed up before we arrived."

"I suppose," Jack conceded reluctantly. "Yeah, you're probably right."

But the creepy sensation refused to fade completely away.

They were making their cautious way around the perimeter of the outpost before Draycos spoke again. "Where are we going?"

"Weren't you listening?" Jack asked. "We're going to

find a transport, you're going to knock out whatever guards there are, and we're going to whistle up the *Essenay*."

"We are leaving, then?"

Jack grimaced. "Look, Draycos, I'm sorry," he said. "It just didn't work out. We'll back off, regroup, and try to get the Djinn-90 data some other way."

"I was not thinking about the information," Draycos said. "I was thinking about those still in Shamshir hands."

"What about them?"

"Did you intend to simply leave them there?"

Jack frowned down at the dragon padding soundlessly through the dead leaves at his side. Uh-oh. "Hey, I know how you feel about that sort of thing," he said cautiously. "K'da warrior ethic, and all that. But I think that asking Colonel Elkor for a rescue party is pretty much out of the question."

"Certainly," Draycos agreed. "That means we will have to do it alone."

Jack took a careful breath. "Look," he said, as if talking to a very small child. "I know you're upset. But you have to understand the realities of the situation. We're talking about two of us—you and me—against a whole mercenary force."

"Dahtill City is not a military base," Draycos pointed out. "There will be a limit on the number of soldiers to oppose us."

"Unless they brought in more after our escape," Jack countered. "They could have, you know."

"If more soldiers were summoned, it would be to search for you outside the city," the dragon pointed out reasonably. "Not to reinforce those inside."

Jack clenched his teeth. This was not going well at all. "We hardly even know these kids," he said. "Anyway, it's Alison's fault they're there, not mine."

"Fault is of no matter," Draycos said. "They are your comrades. Your fellow soldiers. A warrior does not simply abandon those of his own side. Not when there is a chance of saving them."

"Even if it means getting killed?" Jack shot back harshly. "We could, you know. Those guns of theirs weren't just for show. We go charging in, and they're going to start shooting. What happens to your people then? Hmm?"

For a long minute they walked in silence. "Do you remember our first meeting, Jack?" Draycos asked at last. "Despite your objections, I took the time to aid a wounded soldier of the other side."

"You kept him from burning his hands and neck in hot dirt," Jack said, grimacing at the memory. "And I still think it was a waste of time."

"The point is that a warrior does that which is right," the dragon said. "Not because he may profit from it. Because it is right."

"What if I say no?" Jack challenged. "Are you going to go in without me?"

Draycos didn't answer, and after a moment Jack sighed. "You got a plan?"

"I do not believe it will be difficult," Draycos said. "As you pointed out, neither side wishes to risk a serious battle near the daublite mine. With two armed vehicles, we may be able to persuade them to surrender the prisoners without a fight."

It could work, Jack realized grudgingly. Particularly if Lieutenant Cue Ball had already discovered that none of the squad could do anything with the stolen computers. There wouldn't be much point in hanging onto them. "You mentioned two transports. You planning on flying the second one yourself?"

"I actually referred to only one transport," Draycos said. "The other armed vehicle will be the *Essenay*."

"And how do you expect to call in Uncle Virge without everyone from here to Dahtill City knowing the plan?"

"You may leave that to me," Draycos said. "Will you assist me?"

Jack sniffed. "Do I have a choice?"

"Yes," Draycos said quietly. "You are my host. If you refuse to help me rescue the others, I will honor your wishes."

"That's part of the warrior ethic, too, I suppose?"

"Yes."

They walked a few more steps in silence. "You're going to make a liar of me, you know," Jack finally said in resignation. "I told Colonel Elkor we weren't going to steal his transport. Now we're going to do it anyway."

"Do not worry," Draycos assured him. "When you made that statement, it was indeed the truth. There was no intent to deceive. Hence, there was no lie."

Jack looked down at him. "That was supposed to be a joke."

The dragon turned his green eyes upward, his jaws opening slightly. "Yes, I know," he said. "Shall we go?"

Jack shook his head. "Lead the way."

CHAPTER 24

There were two soldiers standing guard beside the Lynx transports when Jack and Draycos arrived at the edge of the clearing. Two minutes later, the guards were no longer standing.

"Can you start the engines?" Draycos asked as Jack dropped into the pilot's seat.

"I think so," Jack said, studying the control board. "But it'll take a couple of minutes. This pilot was smart enough to lock it down before he left."

"Your sewer-rat technique?"

"A version of it, yes," Jack said, keying in the program and then taking a moment to peer out the cockpit windscreen. So far there weren't any other Edgemen in sight. But that could change at any time.

"What about communications?"

"The comm isn't locked," Jack said doubtfully. "But I still don't know how you're going to tell Uncle Virge anything without bringing the whole Shamshir army down on top of us."

"You shall see," Draycos said. "Will you make the correct settings?"

Jack reached over and tuned the equipment to his comm clip's frequency. "Okay, it's set," he said, pointing to the microphone switch. "Punch that, and you're on the air."

"Understood," Draycos said, leaning his torso up onto the control board. "You must stay quiet while I speak. Both Shamshir and Whinyard's Edge listeners may recognize your voice."

Jack nodded. "Got it."

Reaching over, Draycos touched the switch. "Until the brave achieve their rest," he called, his voice deep and formal, "the warrior must put forth his best. And to the last our home defend."

Jack blinked. He knew that tone. Knew it all too well. It was the rather pretentious style Draycos liked to use when reciting his poetry.

What in the world was he doing?

Uncle Virge must have been wondering that, too. For a handful of seconds there was no response. Then, to Jack's amazement, the computer's voice came over the speaker, in the same overbearing tone. "The warfire blazes all around, the killing fields do beckon," he announced. "By curve or straight-line reckon?"

"The dog tells all; the fires blast," Draycos responded. "Until the fury's spent at last."

There was another pause, a longer one this time. "You speak in riddles in my ear," Uncle Virge said. "While all is dark and dank and drear, how can one silence fears unseen?"

"By what foul deed is treason learned?" Draycos came

back. "By what hand are we crushed? The fields and vine-yards hushed."

"They held it strong against our might," Uncle Virge said. "But through the desert we did go, and took it ere the fall of night."

"The scoffers say we face the night," Draycos came back. "That none shall from that road return. The scoffer's words and fears I spurn."

"The world will tremble, warns the foe," Uncle Virge said. "And all will fall like burning leaves. To stand, though none endure to grieve."

With a delicate flick of his claw, Draycos shut off the comm. "How soon may we leave?" he asked.

Jack had been staring at the dragon in fascination. Now, with an effort, he tore his eyes away and found the status board. "Uh . . . we're ready now, looks like."

"Then let us be away," Draycos said. "The *Essenay* will meet us at Dahtill City."

Jack cut in the lifters, and the transport started up into the night sky. No one appeared at the edge of the clearing as he cleared the treetops, shouting at him to come back. Even better, no one showed up and started shooting.

The nav system included a map of the local area. Jack studied it a moment, then turned the transport's nose toward Dahtill City. He did a quick sensor scan of the sky around them, but no one was visible there, either. Apparently, everyone was still out searching for him.

"We are on course?" Draycos asked.

"Sure," Jack said, leaning back in his seat and looking over at the dragon. "Okay, I give up. What in the name of self-buttering brussels sprouts was *that* all about?"

"I was giving him information on our destination," the dragon said blandly. "Did I not say I would do so?"

"Don't be cute," Jack growled. "It's not a good night for it. Just tell me what you did."

Draycos ducked his head. "My apologies. As I have mentioned, I have been translating my poetry into your language and reciting it to Uncle Virge."

Jack frowned, thinking back over the conversation he'd just heard. It had sounded like poetry, all right. But there had been something wrong with it. Something odd about the pacing, or the flow, or the rhyme scheme . . .

And then it hit him. "You were missing a line," he said. "Each stanza of the poem was missing a line."

Draycos's neck arched. "Very good," he said. "I am impressed."

"Thank you," Jack said, rather pleased by it himself. "And the missing line was the message?"

"Exactly," Draycos said. "The complete first stanza that I spoke should have been: 'Until the brave achieve their rest, the warrior must put forth his best. Come here to me, my oldest friend, and to the last our home defend.'"

Jack thought back. "The third line was missing," he said. " 'Come here to me, my oldest friend.' "

"Correct," Draycos said. "Uncle Virge is not precisely my oldest friend, but it was the closest line I knew to what we needed."

"Definitely close enough," Jack agreed. "Especially since he's pretty much *my* oldest friend. What about the others? Uncle Virge said something next about warfire?"

" 'The warfire blazes all around, the killing fields do beckon,' " Draycos recited. " 'How shall my warrior friend be found? By curve or straight-line reckon?' "

" 'How shall my warrior friend be found,' " Jack repeated the missing line. "He wanted to know where we were."

"Correct," Draycos said. "As you can see, he understood quickly what I was doing."

"Uncle Virgil always was a smart old fox," Jack agreed. "Your next one was shorter, wasn't it?"

"Yes," Draycos said. "It was the only one that did not come from one of my poems. I created it on the moment to identify the place where we were headed."

Jack gazed out at the stars, thinking back. *The dog tells all; the fires blast. Until the fury's spent at last.* It didn't make any more sense to him the second time around than it had the first. "You got me," he said.

"Think of the words," Draycos suggested. "Think of where we are going."

"I still don't—" Jack broke off. "You're not serious. 'Dog tells'? Dahtill? Dahtill City?"

"It was the best I could create," Draycos said apologetically. "I hoped he would understand."

"I guess he didn't," Jack said. "You still had a lot more to say to each other."

"True," the dragon conceded. "His next stanza was a question. 'You speak in riddles in my ear. What do you say, what do you mean? While all is dark and dank and drear, how can one silence fears unseen?'"

"'What do you say, what do you mean?'" Jack murmured. "I don't blame him."

"I then tried to give him a useful clue," Draycos said. "'By what foul deed is treason learned? By what hand are we crushed? The mines collapse, the cities burned, the fields and vineyards hushed.'"

"The mines collapse, the cities burned," Jack said, nodding. "A city with a mine beside it."

"He understood then, but was not absolutely certain," Draycos said. "'We sought the city of our foe. They held it strong against our might. But through the desert we did go, and took it ere the fall of night.'"

"The city of our foe," Jack said. "That covers Dahtill City, all right, and probably fifty others along with it."

"But no other is so near to us," Draycos pointed out. "And none that I know of is associated with an important mine. At any rate, I told him he was correct. 'The scoffers say we face the night, that none shall from that road return. But I say that your word is right; the scoffer's words and fears I spurn.'"

But I say that your word is right. "I just hope he really did get the dog-tell pun."

"We shall soon find out," Draycos agreed. "At any rate, he then told me he was leaving."

"'The world will tremble, warns the foe,'" Jack quoted, just to show he could do it. "'And all will fall like burning leaves.' Next?"

"'But I must to my friends now go,'" Draycos supplied the missing line. "'To stand, though none endure to grieve.'"

For a moment the cockpit was silent. "Well, if it *doesn't* work, it sure should have," Jack concluded. "Pretty classy."

"Thank you," the dragon said.

"You're welcome," Jack said. "I hope you've got an equally clever plan for getting the others out."

"Actually . . ."

Jack eyed him. "You don't, do you?"

"It is difficult to plan with so many variables," the dragon hedged. "We do not know where our enemies will be positioned."

"I thought they were all going to be out looking for me," Jack reminded him.

"Some may be," Draycos agreed. "But others will have stayed behind. At any rate, even the searchers may have returned by this time."

"In other words, you're going to wing it."

The tip of the dragon's tail twitched. "That is not precisely how I would have phrased it," he said. "But it is basically accurate."

Jack sighed. "I thought so."

CHAPTER 25

With Dahtill City five more minutes away, Jack took the Lynx down to treetop height. "I take it we're not jumping out this time?" he asked Draycos.

"Correct," Draycos called from the back, where he was rummaging through the various storage lockers. "We may require this vehicle to move the prisoners. Is its ventral armor as strong as that of the Flying Turtle we used earlier?"

"They're similar models, so probably," Jack said. Not that any amount of armor would do them any good if the Shamshir knocked out the lifters. "Any luck back there?"

"Very little," Draycos reported. "The soldiers must have taken most of the weapons with them on their search for you. I have found only two small MP-50 machine guns, with two spare clips each."

Killing weapons, the kind Jack had spent his life avoiding. "Nothing else?" he asked. "No sopor gas or slapsticks or anything like that?"

"The only other weapons are nine Class II explosive grenades," Draycos said. "There are no nonlethal weapons of the sort you prefer. I am sorry."

Jack grimaced. "Me, too. Well, I guess we'll have to do

what we can. Maybe we can just pin the Shamshir down while Uncle Virge swoops in and—"

"What was that?" Draycos cut him off.

Jack threw a quick look toward the horizon, then checked his sensor displays. There was nothing unusual that he could see. "What was what?"

"A small flash of light directly ahead," Draycos said, covering the length of the transport in two bounds to land at Jack's side. "There—it came again."

"I didn't see anything," Jack said, learning forward and staring out into the night. "What did it look like?"

"Like the discharge of a Gompers flash rifle," Draycos said. "As if far in the distance—"

And then, faintly, it came again. A flicker of light, like a small flash of lightning coming from below the horizon. "You mean like that?" Jack asked.

"Exactly," Draycos said. "There—another."

"Someone's doing some shooting," Jack muttered, watching the flashes. "A *lot* of shooting."

"The Shamshir would not execute their prisoners, would they?" Draycos asked, his voice dark and ominous.

"I hope not," Jack said, studying the flickers of light. There didn't seem to be any pattern to them, no nice neat one-two-three sequence. "Anyway, that doesn't look like a firing squad."

"Then there is a battle," Draycos concluded. "I will fly. You will shoot."

"Wait a second," Jack objected. "I will shoot what?"

"We will know when we arrive," Draycos said, nudging

Jack impatiently with the side of his head. "Go. You must prepare."

"But the *Essenay*'s not here yet."

"We have no choice," Draycos said firmly. "We must see what is happening. Go."

Reluctantly, Jack climbed out of the pilot's seat. "I don't like this," he said. "Why don't we land someplace near the city and take a quiet look instead of charging blindly in?"

"There is no time," Draycos said, sliding into Jack's seat and gripping the controls with his paws. "Whether the Agri are fighting the Shamshir, or whether the Whinyard's Edge has launched their own strike, we cannot afford a delay."

"What makes you think that?"

"Call it warrior's instinct." Draycos turned his green eyes on Jack, "Go. Prepare."

"Terrific," Jack muttered, heading aft to where Draycos had laid out the MP-50s. Why the Agri should suddenly have risen up against the Shamshir he couldn't imagine. And the idea that the Edge would have gotten involved was completely ridiculous.

Unless they'd gone to Dahtill City looking for him. Maybe Colonel Elkor was madder at getting stuck up that tree than he'd thought.

He reached the back and picked up one of the MP-50s. For such a relatively small gun, it was awfully heavy. Fortunately, Draycos had already loaded the ammo clip into it, since Jack couldn't remember exactly how to do that. "Any particular side you want me on?" he called.

"Use the right-hand side," Draycos said.

"Okay." Grabbing two spare clips and stuffing them into his jacket pockets, he crossed to the right-hand hatchway.

Unlike the Flying Turtle they'd escaped in earlier, the Lynx had a pair of safety harnesses attached to the bulkhead beside each of the side hatches. Designed for soldiers to use while shooting outside, he decided as he slipped one of them on and tightened it into place. "How am I supposed to know what to shoot at?" he called to Draycos.

"I will direct your fire," the dragon said. "We have cleared the last trees now and are approaching the city from the south-west. Prepare."

Taking a deep breath, Jack got a firm grip on his gun and hit the hatchway release. The panel slid up into the ceiling, and for the second time that night he found himself standing at the edge of a hurricane.

He took another deep breath, his mind flashing back to some of the stupider jobs he and Uncle Virgil had pulled when he was little. Back then, he'd often felt himself standing just like this, balanced at the edge of disaster, waiting for Uncle Virgil to give the signal. Wondering the whole time whether either of them would be alive to see another sunrise.

Here, the sun wouldn't be up for at least a couple more hours. He wondered if he would be alive to see it.

And then, from the cockpit, he heard a startled bark. "What?" he demanded, his heartbeat suddenly thudding extra hard in his throat.

"They are free," Draycos called back. "Observe." He

twisted the transport around, sending Jack swinging on his harness halfway out the hatchway.

And as he hung balanced there, he was treated to a bird's-eye view of an amazing scene.

Directly ahead was the landing area at the edge of the city, the one he and Draycos had escaped from. The two Flying Turtles he'd left behind were still there, facing the two Shamshir buildings. From the windows of those buildings a hail of machine gun bullets was blasting out at one of the transports, accompanied by an occasional flash of laser fire.

And at the focus of all that fury, firing gamely back at their attackers, was the rest of Technical Squad Tango Five Zulu.

Jommy and Li were crouched in the open hatchway, Jommy with some kind of machine gun, Li firing blasts with a Gompers flash rifle. Below them, lying flat on the ground behind one of the transport's landing skids, were Rogan and Brinkster, also with machine guns.

Alison was nowhere in sight, but it wasn't hard to guess where she was. Ten to one she was already inside the transport, trying to get it started.

Jack shook his head, half amazed, half annoyed. Here he'd come all this way back to rescue them, and they'd already gotten out on their own.

"You must give covering fire," Draycos called from the cockpit.

Jack took another look. The dragon was right. The squad

was fighting back well enough, but unless Alison could get the Flying Turtle started real soon, they were going to run out of ammunition long before the Shamshir gave up and went away. "Right," he called back between clenched teeth. "What do I do?"

A second later he was thrown back inside as the dragon swung them around in a tight circle. Just in time; even as he grabbed for a strap to steady himself, a burst of gunfire raked across the side of the transport, some of the rounds chewing up the ceiling and far wall. "Stay clear!" Draycos shouted.

"You bet," Jack ground out, suddenly remembering what exactly it was he had gotten himself into. This wasn't some practice drill, and those Shamshir soldiers out there weren't firing marker lasers.

Draycos straightened the Lynx out, and Jack pulled himself cautiously back to the door. They had overshot the scene of the battle, he saw, and were coming back around behind the buildings. Apparently Draycos meant for him to shoot at the Shamshir from behind.

That was fine with him. He'd just as soon fire from a direction the other guys' guns weren't pointed at. He flipped the firing lever like the Whinyard's Edge manual had showed, pointed the gun in the general direction of the buildings, and pulled the trigger.

If it hadn't been for the harness holding him up, he would have instantly found himself flat on his back. As it was, he nearly wound up there anyway. The MP-50 had a kick like an angry Brummga, a hundred times more powerful than the simple little tangler gun he was used to.

The weapon also had a definite mind of its own. Even as he staggered backward, the muzzle seemed to jump upward, and before he could get his finger off the trigger his burst had chewed up a little more of the transport's ceiling.

"Jack!"

"I'm okay," Jack called back, struggling back to his feet and trying to salvage some shreds of dignity. "I've never fired one of these things, that's all."

"Come up here," Draycos ordered. "You will fly. I will shoot."

So much for dignity. So much, too, for any possible career as a soldier. Just in case he'd been interested in one. "Sure," Jack muttered, untangling himself from his harness and running forward.

They were nearly back to the edge of the forest now, Jack saw as Draycos hopped out of the pilot's seat and he hopped in. "What do you want me to do?" he asked.

"Take us behind the Shamshir buildings," Draycos instructed. Snatching the MP-50 from Jack's hands, he headed aft, loping along on three legs as he hugged the machine gun to his belly with the other.

"Right," Jack said, sending the transport around again in a smooth curve. He caught a glimpse of the darkened mine buildings as he swung past, and then they were sweeping back toward the firefight.

There was a fresh sound of wind behind him. He glanced back, saw that Draycos had opened the left-hand hatchway door and was crouching beside it. "Better use the safety harness," Jack called.

"I will be all right," the dragon replied. "Just keep your flight movements smooth."

Jack turned back to his flying, feeling his stomach trying hard to turn itself inside out. Now that the element of surprise was gone, the Shamshir weren't going to just sit there and let the intruder take potshots at them.

And indeed, the transport's bow and windscreen were already starting to crackle with the impact of bullets. Biting down hard on his lip, trying to remember Draycos's optimistic assumptions about the Lynx's armor, he forced himself to ignore the deadly hail and to keep his head high enough to see where he was going. From the rear he could hear the chatter of Draycos's gun as they buzzed past the building.

And then, even as he cautiously lifted his head, the landscape ahead of him suddenly flared with light.

For that first awful second, he thought the Shamshir had blown up the Flying Turtle, killing the rest of his squad. Heart pounding in his ears, he swung the Lynx around.

It hadn't been the Flying Turtle that had blown up. Instead, it was one of the Agri hardened-mud huts that was now blazing furiously away. The very hut, in fact, that he'd been locked into after his little chat with Lieutenant Cue Ball.

The hut that had contained, among other things, grenades and spare ammunition.

"Did it work?" Draycos asked. He was at Jack's side now, peering over his shoulder.

"I don't know," Jack said. "How exactly was it *supposed* to work?"

The dragon's tongue flicked out. "Like so."

To Jack's amazement, the Shamshir soldiers were on the move. Not toward the transport, like they had decided to rush it, but away.

All of them. Running away from the two buildings like the whole Whinyard's Edge was after them.

Jack cleared his throat. "You think they're running because of the risk of burning explosives next door?" he asked carefully.

"Of course," Draycos said, a distinct note of satisfaction in his voice.

"Not maybe because there might be something else in the hut?" Jack went on. "Something maybe a little nastier than grenades?"

"I—" Draycos broke off. "I do not know."

"Me, neither," Jack said grimly. "What do you say we get the squad aboard and get out of here?"

"Agreed," Draycos said. Setting his gun onto the deck, he leaped up and vanished down the back of Jack's shirt. "And Jack?"

"Yes?"

The dragon's head rose a little from his shoulder. "Do not land us too close to the fire. Just in case."

CHAPTER 26

Jack put the Lynx down between the burning hut and the squad's chosen Flying Turtle. "Jommy?" he shouted through the open hatchway before stepping into view. "It's Jack Montana. Don't shoot."

"Okay," Jommy called back. "Come on."

Jack hopped down from the door. "Everyone okay?" he called as he hurried toward them.

"So far," Jommy grunted. "Though if Kayna can't get this thing started, that could change real fast."

"I told him it was you," Rogan piped up. The smaller boy was shaking where he lay, but he held his gun bravely at the ready. "I told him. He didn't believe me."

"Don't worry, I wouldn't have believed you, either," Jack said, jerking his head back toward his transport. "Come on—everybody get aboard and let's get out of here."

"We won't get far in that one," Li warned. She gestured over Jack's shoulder with the muzzle of her Gompers. "They got your tanks."

Jack turned and looked. Sure enough, there was a ragged gash in the side of the transport that was leaking fuel like a miniature waterfall. "We'll have to take yours, then," he said. "You said Alison's in there?"

"Yeah," Jommy said, glancing around. "She *said* she could get it started."

"I'll give her a hand," Jack said, slinging his MP-50 over his shoulder. "Keep a sharp eye. When the Shamshir ran off, I don't think they were really giving up."

He found Alison in the pilot's seat, muttering darkly at the control board. "How's it going?" Jack asked, coming up beside her.

"It's frozen solid," she growled, throwing him a curious look. "So you came back, huh?"

"That's the rumor, anyway," Jack said, leaning over her shoulder to try a couple of keys. It was frozen, all right. "What have you tried?"

"What, are you an expert on computer systems?"

"On breaking into them, yes," Jack shot back, trying to think. The good news was that the computer setup was probably similar to the Edge system he'd successfully hacked into on the leaking shuttle out there.

The bad news was that whatever Alison had done to it, she'd probably locked it down so tight that his sewer-rat trick wouldn't work.

Which left them only one option. "We need the start key," he told her, turning and heading aft. "There ought to be a copy on one of the computers in the Shamshir HQ. I'll go get it."

She was at his side before he even got to the hatchway. "I'll go with you," she said, snatching up a machine gun from the floor.

"Forget it," he said, throwing her an annoyed glare. There was a fair chance there were still some soldiers lurking in the building, and the last thing he wanted was to have Draycos's freedom of action cramped by the presence of an unwelcome witness. "Stay here and—"

"And what?" she cut him off. "It won't start. Anyway, two soldiers together always have a better chance than one."

Jack grimaced. That was probably true . . . except when one of them had a K'da warrior on his back.

They made it to the HQ building's outer door without anyone shooting at them. The distant mud hut, Jack noted uneasily, seemed to be burning even more furiously than it had been when he'd first landed. He wondered what the blast range was of the grenades Draycos had spotted in there.

"I'll go first," Alison said. Without waiting for argument she ducked inside. Setting his teeth firmly together, Jack followed.

No one shot at them in here, either. In fact, for all they could tell, the whole place was indeed deserted. "I don't like this," Jack murmured as they eased along the darkened corridor. "They shouldn't *all* have run. Should they?"

"Depends on what they were running from," Alison said. "Or maybe what they were running *to*."

"Meaning?"

"Meaning maybe they're afraid of something in that shed you torched," she said, peering around an open doorway and then moving on. "Or maybe they just decided on a tactical retreat."

"Like I said: meaning?" Jack repeated, starting to feel

annoyed again. This wasn't any time to be playing word games.

"Meaning maybe they didn't feel like facing a bunch of Edge combat transports all alone." She glanced over her shoulder. "There *are* more transports on the way, aren't there?"

Jack shook his head. "Sorry."

Alison's forehead creased, but she merely turned back and continued on. "Well, the Shamshir don't know that," she pointed out. "I just hope they don't have any air power of their own on the way. Though they probably do."

She paused at another doorway and looked in. "Here we go," she said, and went inside.

The room was small and bare of any ornamentation, Jack noted as he slipped in behind her. But from the size of the desk, and the amount of padding on the chair, it looked like they'd found the commanding officer's office.

With a nice little computer humming away on a corner of the desk.

Alison made a beeline for the computer. Jack brushed past her elbow and got there first. "Uh-uh," he said firmly, setting his gun down on the desk and dropping into the chair. "You already messed up the transport's computer. This one's mine."

She made as if to object, hesitated, then nodded. "Fine," she said, going back to the doorway and peering cautiously down the hall with her machine gun ready. "You just better know what you're doing."

"Trust me," Jack said, testing the keys. The computer was still running, but the owner had remembered to lock it down before making his tactical retreat. Sewer-rat time. "It'll take a few minutes," he added, keying in the program.

"Not too many, I hope," she said. "So if you aren't leading a charge, what *are* you doing here?"

"I came to get you guys out," Jack said. "Or are you going to try to tell me you didn't need any help?"

"I never turn down free help," she told him tightly. "Especially right now. If we can't get that transport started, it's going to be a long walk to anywhere."

"With unhappy Shamshir behind us the whole way," Jack agreed. "Boy, I'd hate to be in our shoes. How'd you get out, anyway?"

There was just the slightest pause. "The hut they put me in had a dirt floor," she said. "They'd fastened the other end of my handcuffs to the leg of one of the shelves."

"Same thing they did to me," Jack said. "Not very imaginative, are they?"

"Hey, whatever works," she said with a shrug. "Anyway, all I had to do was dig enough dirt out from under the leg, and I could slip the handcuff right out. Nice and neat."

"Yeah," Jack said, frowning. Nice and neat, all right.

Except that when they'd locked *him* up, they'd made sure the handcuff was attached above the bottom shelf. How had she managed to get that shelf unfastened? "And then you just went around and popped the others?"

"More or less," she said. "How about you?" I notice *you* even managed to get yourself a transport."

Jack snorted gently. "I have friends."

She frowned across the room at him. "And?"

"That's all," he said. "I have friends."

"What sort of friends does an Edgeman have in a Shamshir camp?"

"You'd be surprised," Jack said. The computer was coming loose now, and he keyed for a directory. "Anyway, you've got as good a chance of finding friends here right now as you do in the Whinyard's Edge."

"Meaning?"

"Meaning it turns out our group was thrown to the wolves." He looked up and caught her eyes in a hard stare. "Thanks to you and your little midnight visit to the Edge HQ back on Carrion."

Her lip twitched. "So they knew about that."

"Not only did they know about it, they decided to fry your whole circle of friends along with you," Jack told her. "What were you doing there that night, anyway?"

"Looking for some information."

"What kind?"

"The kind that's none of your business," she said tartly. "Aren't you supposed to be breaking into a computer or something?"

"Patience, dear, patience," Jack said. Scrolling down the pilot/aircraft listing, he found the Flying Turtle section. The computerized start key . . . there it was. "Here we go," he said, grabbing a data tube from a stack beside the computer and popping it in. He keyed for copy, there was a brief hum, and the data tube popped back out. "Got it," he announced, standing up.

And then, even as he started toward Alison, a strange

thought suddenly struck him. He stopped, his eyes flicking back to the computer . . .

"What's wrong?" Alison asked.

"Nothing," Jack said, flipping the tube to her. "Go get it started. I'll be right there."

She caught the tube, her expression suddenly wary. "What kind of heroics are you thinking about *now*?"

"The kind that are none of your business," he said. "Go on, get out. That air support could be here any time."

Alison's mouth compressed tightly, but she nodded. "Don't take too long," she warned, and vanished down the hall.

"Jack?" Draycos murmured from Jack's shoulder. "What are you doing?"

"Completing my primary mission, as you warrior types would say," Jack said, sitting back down at the computer. "Or did you forget why we came here in the first place?"

The dragon's head rose up out of his jacket. "The Djinn-90 information?"

"Why not?" Jack said, keying for a new directory. "Unless you're finicky about which mercenary group we get it from."

"I do not know that word." With a bound, the dragon leaped from Jack's back, landing halfway to the door. "But the meaning is clear. I will stand guard."

"Good idea," Jack said absently, his full attention on the screen. Okay; there were the Shamshir's own records. But where were the ones they kept on other groups? Surely they kept records on other groups.

"Jack?"

"I'm hurrying, I'm hurrying," Jack growled. Finally, there it was. Now all he had to do was find the section on aircraft . . .

"Jack, we must go," Draycos insisted, his tone suddenly urgent. "We must go *now*."

Jack looked up. The dragon was standing at the door, his tongue flicking in and out with the speed of a blackjack dealer throwing cards. "What is it?" he asked, reaching for his gun.

"The taste of death," Draycos said. "Coming from the fire."

CHAPTER 27

Cautiously, Jack sniffed at the air. His own nose couldn't find anything other than simple basic smoke. "Are you sure?"

"I have tasted many such poisons before," Draycos said, his voice even more urgent. "Come."

Jack looked back at the computer, a tight feeling in the pit of his stomach. No—this couldn't be happening. Not twice on the same job. To have come this close—again!—only to get chased away before he could finish it?

"Jack!" Draycos called.

And then, like one of Uncle Virgil's dope-slaps on the side of his head, the obvious answer struck him.

If there wasn't time to pick and choose what he wanted, he would just take everything.

"Thirty seconds," he promised Draycos, grabbing another tube and jamming it into the receptacle. "Make sure the coast is clear," he added, keying for a complete copy of the Shamshir's rival mercenary data lists.

And then, with a terrific concussion, the whole building seemed to lift itself up and drop back onto the ground.

"What was that?" Jack yelled. At least, he thought he

yelled it. With his ears ringing from the blast, he couldn't even hear his own voice.

Draycos was at his side, mouthing something. "What?" Jack shouted back.

In answer, the dragon hooked the claws of one of his forepaws into Jack's jacket sleeve and tugged him toward the door. "Wait a second," Jack said, reaching over and popping the data tube.

Just in time. Even as he pulled the tube free, the building's power shut down, taking the computer with it. Draycos tugged again. "Right," Jack agreed, shoving the data tube deep into an inner pocket. "Let's go."

He fully expected there to be another blast or two along the way. But they reached the outer door without that happening. Jack peered outside, started to step through the doorway—

And found himself yanked back inside by the claws still hooked into his sleeve as a dark aircraft roared past overhead.

Reflexively, he dropped into a crouch. "Uh-oh," he muttered.

"We are under attack," he heard Draycos's voice distantly through his slowly recovering hearing.

"No kidding, Sherlock," Jack said, looking carefully around the door jamb. In the flickering light of the burning hut, the Lynx transport he'd arrived in seemed intact. Or at least as intact as it had been when he'd left it. Beyond it . . .

He tensed. Beyond the Lynx, where Tango Five Zulu's borrowed Flying Turtle had been, there was nothing but a gaping crater.

"There," Draycos said, pointing a claw. "They are there."

Jack looked. In the near distance he could see the shape of the Flying Turtle scooting across the sky.

So Alison had managed to get the thing started and into the air. And not a borrowed second too soon, either, from the looks of it. "Who else is around?" he asked.

"I can hear two Shamshir fighter craft," Draycos said. "Both are in pursuit of Alison's vehicle."

"Okay," Jack said, getting back to his feet again. "Let's see if we can make it to the Lynx."

"It is damaged," Draycos reminded him.

"Would you rather walk away from poison gas?"

"Point," Draycos conceded, putting a paw on Jack's hand and slithering up his sleeve. "Let us go."

Again, they made it across the open area without drawing fire. Apparently, none of Lieutenant Cue Ball's men wanted him badly enough to stick around near the burning hut. "We're not going to get very far," he warned, glancing at the fuel reading as he dropped into the pilot's seat. "But we should at least make it to the woods."

The comm beeped. "Montana?" Alison's voice came.

Jack flipped the switch. "I'm here," he confirmed. "You all right?"

"Oh, we're just sweetness and light out here," she growled back. "Sorry, but we had to pull out. If I can shake these two birds, I'll circle back and get you."

"No, don't," Jack said. "You just stay ahead of them and head for the hills. I can get out on my own."

"But—"

And suddenly, outside the windscreen, the ground flashed with light. Jack leaned forward over the control board, trying to see what had happened.

One of the Shamshir fighters had become an airborne fireball.

Jack blinked. No. Not even Alison. Not even Alison and Jommy together, hotshot teenage mercenaries that they were, could have taken out a professional combat pilot. Could they?

And then, even as his brain tried to make sense of it, the second fighter veered away from its prey. It cut hard to the left, its guns blazing full power, and exploded into a fireball of its own.

"Jack?" a familiar voice called.

Jack felt his breath go out of him in a whoosh, his muscles going limp with relief.

He'd forgotten all about Uncle Virge.

"I'm here, Uncle Virge," he called back. "On the ground, in the Lynx near the burning hut. Leave the Flying Turtle alone—they're on our side. Anyone else in the area?"

"Looks like they've got three more fighters coming in from the south," Uncle Virge reported. "Still a few minutes away. Pretty amateurish for supposed professionals, if you want my humble opinion."

"They weren't expecting to have to fight around here," Jack said, gazing thoughtfully out the windscreen into the distance. An idea was starting to form in the back of his mind.

"I'm coming in to get you," Uncle Virge said. "Did you know that fire is putting out xancrene gas?"

"Yeah, I did, thanks," Jack said, keying on the engines. "On second thought, I'll meet you two miles west of the city."

"There's no need for that, Jack lad," Uncle Virge protested. "I wouldn't trust that flying cattle car of yours farther than I can bounce a barge. Don't worry; the xancrene is mostly blowing north."

"I wasn't worried about the xancrene," Jack told him, lifting the transport into the air. "And relax, this thing will get me far enough."

"Jack lad—"

"Look, I know what I'm doing," Jack interrupted him. "Alison? You still there?"

"Still here," she confirmed. "Thanks for the assist."

"Like I said, I have friends," Jack said. "Look, I'd ask you all aboard, but we really don't have the space. I'm afraid you'll have to find your own way off Sunright."

"That's okay," she assured him. "We'll manage."

"The Edge will be watching for you," he warned.

"Like I said, we'll manage," she said. "I have friends, too. See you."

The comm clicked off. "Yeah," Jack muttered, her last words tingling across his mind. *I have friends too . . .*

He headed off into the night. Directly ahead, the dim lights of the mine buildings loomed against the darkness.

The mine that had sparked all this trouble in the first place. The mine that had trapped both the Agri and the

Parprins into devil's bargains with greedy mercenaries. The jackpot both the Shamshir and Whinyard's Edge were playing their deadly little games for.

As Uncle Virgil would have said, it was time to take the jackpot off the table.

He lined up the transport's nose on the entrance to the main mine building. "Draycos, you said there were some grenades back there?"

"Yes," Draycos said. "Nine of them."

"I don't suppose you'd know how to rig a delay fuse on something like that."

"Explosives are not to be dealt with lightly or casually," the dragon said, his voice starting to sound suspicious. "I am not trained with these particular devices."

"Never mind, then," Jack said. "We'll do it the old-fashioned way. Can you get them out of the locker and line them up along the floor? Straight down the middle should do just fine."

Draycos's head lifted up from Jack's shoulder. "Jack, what is it you intend to do?"

Jack nodded toward the mine buildings. "The Shamshir want the mine," he said. "So do the Whinyard's Edge, if you believe Lieutenant Cue Ball. What do you suppose they'd do if the mine wasn't there anymore?"

Draycos pondered a moment. "Those who care only for its wealth would leave this world."

He twisted his head around to look squarely into Jack's eyes. "But this is not your property, Jack," he added. "You have no right to choose its destruction."

"Not even to save people caught in a war none of them want?" Jack countered. "Come on, K'da warrior, let's hear those ethics of yours. Is the wealth from a mine more important than the people who own it?"

"The people are of course more important," the dragon said, his voice oddly sad. "But there must be another way."

"There isn't," Jack said firmly. "Look, I trust you in warrior stuff. Trust me in this, okay?"

Draycos bounded from Jack's collar, landing on the deck behind him. "Very well," he said reluctantly. "If there is no other way, then let us do it."

Jack smiled tightly. The K'da poet-warrior had done his part of the job. Now it was time for the human con artist to do his. "Just line up those grenades," he said. "I'll do the rest."

The main doors were wide and tall, designed to let large ore-carrying vehicles in and out. They were also built pretty strong.

Fortunately, the Lynx was built even stronger. With a crash of breaking wood and the screech of torn metal, it broke through the doors and rumbled into the main building beyond.

"How are you doing?" Jack shouted over the crunch of demolished support beams and wall siding as he drove the Lynx inward toward the tall tower that stood over the mine opening itself.

"I am nearly ready," Draycos called back.

"Good," Jack said. "Brace yourself."

And with a final thunderous crash, he slammed the transport through the lower part of the tower and settled to the floor squarely on top of the shaft leading down into the ground.

"We're here," Jack announced, shutting off the engines and sliding out of his seat. "Let's make tracks."

Draycos looked up from the neat row of grenades he had laid out from the rear of the compartment to just behind Jack's seat. "Pardon?"

"Let's get out of here," Jack clarified. "Come aboard."

With Draycos on his back, Jack picked his way through the splintered wood and other debris outside. The *Essenay* was waiting just outside the entrance, bobbing slightly on its lifters with an air of worried impatience. "Come on, lad, come on," Uncle Virge urged as Jack ran up the ramp. "Those other fighters will be here any minute."

"Then let's give them something to light their way," Jack said as he raced to the cockpit and slid into the pilot's seat. "I want a quick laser burst straight in the hole we made."

"Targeted where?" Uncle Virge asked.

"Targeted on the back of the transport we made the hole with," Jack said, doing a quick check of the *Essenay*'s weapons systems.

"The transport?" Uncle Virge asked, sounding confused. "But—?"

"Never mind," Jack said. "You just aim. I'll fire."

"We should move back," Draycos murmured. "The blast could be considerable."

"Good point," Jack agreed, keying the *Essenay* into a fast backward drift. "Everyone ready?"

"I suppose," Uncle Virge said. Draycos didn't answer.

"Good," Jack said. "Here goes."

The lasers flickered, and he held his breath. If this didn't work . . .

And then, from the entrance came a flash of return light, then the roiling flicker of fire. The rest of the Lynx's fuel had caught. "That should do it," Jack said, pulling the *Essenay* around and heading for the sky. "Let's grab some distance before the grenades go."

"The *grenades*?" Uncle Virge echoed. "Jack, lad—"

And then, the grenades went.

It was even more spectacular than Jack had expected. The sides of the main building blew out as a ring of fire sliced horizontally outward in all directions. The tower, directly above the explosion, shot probably half a dozen feet straight up, then toppled over. It landed on one of the two side buildings, crashing through its roof.

A few seconds after it had begun, it was over. The buildings had collapsed into shattered ruin, with everything flammable in them burning furiously. It was like one of the triumphal bonfires Jack had read about, except that there was no one here celebrating anything.

Maybe the Agri who had worked so hard to create the mine would thank him. Eventually.

He took a deep breath. "Well," he said, to no one in particular. "I guess that's that."

"It is indeed," Uncle Virge agreed, sounding rather awestruck himself. "Never let it be said that you do things halfway, Jack lad."

Jack pursed his lips. Maybe. Maybe not. For now, he could only hope he'd accomplished what he'd set out to do. "We'd better get out of here before those fighters arrive," he said, reaching for the controls. "You with me, Draycos?"

"I am here," the dragon said softly. "Yes; let us go."

CHAPTER 28

"Sorry, lad," Uncle Virge said, his voice as quiet and apologetic and sincere as a professional fundraiser. "I'm afraid the Shamshir Mercenaries keep pretty sloppy records on their competitors' aircraft. There isn't any way we're going to be able to trace those Djinn-90s from this."

"Uh-huh," Jack said, gazing across the table with a fascinated repugnance as he watched Draycos tearing into his fourth soup bowl full of hamburger, tuna fish, chocolate sauce, and motor oil.

It wasn't that he couldn't understand the dragon's hunger. After all, Draycos hadn't had much to eat for the past three weeks. But the thought of that particular food combination still sent Jack's own taste buds screaming for cover. "So that's it, huh?"

"That's it," Uncle Virge confirmed. "And if I may say so, you might recall that I thought the idea was doomed idiocy from the start. So now we can get on with a proper job of saving Draycos's people?"

"By which you mean turning him over to the Star-Force?" Jack suggested.

Draycos looked up, his long tongue flicking a bit of tuna

fish off one corner of his snout. "We cannot do that, Jack," he protested. "It is too dangerous."

"Relax," Jack said, taking a sip of his fizzy-soda. Yes, Uncle Virge had sounded quiet and apologetic and sincere, all right. Unfortunately for him, Jack had heard that tone of voice before. Many times before. "You know, Draycos, for being such a clever K'da poet-warrior, you're kind of slow on the uptake sometimes."

The dragon's neck arched warningly. "What do you mean?" he asked, his voice ominous.

"Relax," Jack hastened to reassure him. Apparently, the dragon wasn't in a mood for joking. "Watch and learn."

He cleared his throat. "Okay, Uncle Virge," he said. "So we don't have anything on the Djinn-90s. What interesting tidbits *did* you happen to find in the Shamshir data?"

"You only asked for the Djinn-90 information," Uncle Virge reminded him.

"I know what I asked for," Jack said firmly. "Quit stalling. What did you find?"

There was a moment of sulky silence. "There's one small piece that *might* be considered interesting," Uncle Virge conceded at last. "But, really, it's so minuscule—"

"I said quit stalling," Jack interrupted. "Give."

"It's just an item about the Brummgas," Uncle Virge groused. "Remember how you ran into a Brummga on Iota Klestis, at the site of Draycos's crash?"

"Like I'd forget," Jack said with a grimace. If Draycos hadn't used Jack's tangler gun on the big alien, both he and the dragon would have wound up very dead. "And Lieutenant

Cue Ball had a couple on his staff, too, hanging around looking ugly," he added. "So?"

"So at least from the Shamshir data," Uncle Virge said grudgingly, "it looks like all the Brummgas in the various mercenary forces come from the same place."

Jack sat up a little straighter. "What do you mean, the same place?" he asked. "The same city? Same province?"

Uncle Virge sighed audibly. "Same dealer."

Draycos's neck was still arched. "What do you mean by 'dealer'?" he asked.

"I'm not sure," Jack said grimly. "But I can guess. Are you talking about a slave dealer, Uncle Virge?"

"Well, of course, mercenaries are considered skilled labor," Uncle Virge hedged. "And Brummgan law isn't quite, shall we say, up to Internos standards—"

"They deal in slavery," Draycos cut him off.

Uncle Virge sighed again. "Yes."

Draycos hissed like he had a bad taste in his mouth, his neck crest stiffer than Jack had ever seen it. "The indenture of children was barbaric enough," he bit out, his eyes glittering like lasers filtered through a pair of emeralds. "But for intelligent beings to be owned like animals—"

"Easy, pal, easy," Jack said hastily, holding up his hands. "Don't get mad at *me*. Or at the Internos government, for that matter. Like I've told you before, we humans aren't in charge of everything that happens out there."

"What about the Trade Association?" Draycos demanded. "Are there not laws concerning such things?"

"There are some, sure," Jack said. "But you can only

enforce what you can see. And there are only so many Judge-Paladins to go around. Come on—we're trying."

Slowly, the crest softened. "I understand," he murmured. "It is still an abomination."

"No argument there," Jack agreed, shivering. He'd seen a group of slaves on one of the worlds he and Uncle Virgil had visited once. The memory of their haunted eyes and faces had stuck with him ever since. "But in this case, it could be a useful abomination."

"What do you mean?" Draycos asked.

"Nothing good," Uncle Virge cut in. "You can wager your teeth and tail on that. Jack—look, lad—"

"We need to find those mercenaries, Uncle Virge," Jack said. "And since we aren't having any luck tracing their fighters, maybe we can trace their personnel."

"And how do you intend to do that?" Uncle Virge demanded. "How do you expect to get close enough to a Brummga slave lord to get a look at his records?"

"Perhaps as a soldier for hire," Draycos suggested.

"Forget it," Jack said firmly. "I'm not cut out to be a soldier."

"You did not do badly," Draycos said. "Do not forget that you were not properly trained or led. And you were certainly not among true warriors."

"I appreciate the vote of confidence," Jack said dryly. "But I think we'll find a different way in, if it's all the same to you."

"That is your option," Draycos said. "Still, whether you accept it or not, you are showing great progress in living by a warrior's ethic."

Jack snorted gently. "I don't know how you figure that one."

"You told Alison not to risk coming back for you," Draycos reminded him. "That showed your consideration of others' safety before your own."

Jack felt his lip twist. "Well . . . actually, no, it didn't. I just didn't want her bringing the Shamshir chase ships back my direction."

Draycos's tail arched. "Truly?"

Jack shrugged. "Sorry."

Uncle Virge laughed out loud. "That's my boy," he said smugly. "See there, Draycos, old snake? Jack's not as easily corrupted by this warrior ethic nonsense as you'd like to think."

"Perhaps," Draycos said, his eyes seeming to measure Jack. "Perhaps it is merely a path that will require many small steps. Do not forget he *did* return to rescue the others."

"Only because you pressured him, I'd wager," Uncle Virge said. "Like I suppose you also pressured him into wrecking that daublite mine for no good reason."

"I suggested nothing of the sort," Draycos protested. "Furthermore, there *was* a good reason. The Agri had become virtual prisoners of the Shamshir mercenaries they had hired. From all appearances, the Parprins were in same situation with the Whinyard's Edge."

"And whose fault was that?" Uncle Virge shot back. "Theirs, that's whose."

"Is it a fault to work to create a source of profit, only to have it stolen away?" Draycos countered.

"Of course not," Jack put in. "That's as bad as a bunch of

mercenaries trying to steal someone else's property and having a kid come along and con it right out from under them."

The budding argument stopped dead on its rails. "What did you say?" Uncle Virge demanded suspiciously.

"Yes," Draycos seconded. "What did that mean?"

Jack smiled. Yes, his relationship with Draycos was going to change his relationship with Uncle Virge. Maybe it would indeed change it forever, the way he'd wondered and worried about earlier as he stood alone in the darkness of the forest.

But maybe that wasn't such a bad thing. Maybe the three of them together were going to hammer themselves into a better team than he'd ever thought they could be. Certainly a better team than he'd ever dared to hope. "Remember, Uncle Virge, when we were leaving Sunright you said that I didn't do things halfway?" he said. "Well, as a matter of fact . . ."

The thin young man's name was Louie, and he was red-faced and panting as he lugged the two footlockers through the door and into the middle of the run-down hotel room. "Okay," he puffed, dropping the end of the first footlocker onto the floor with a thud. "Yours."

He dropped the second footlocker with an equally loud thud. "His."

"You sure it's the right one?" Alison Kayna asked, glancing both ways down the hallway before closing the door behind him.

"The name tag says 'Jack Montana' in big letters," Louie pointed out. "I deserve a bonus for this one, kiddo."

"What for, lugging and handling charges?" Alison countered scornfully. "Come on, be real. The way I hear it, the Whinyard's Edge was pulling off Sunright so fast the whole base was running in ten directions at once. You could have loaded one of their own Lynxes with goodies and flown it out without anyone noticing."

"Busy or not, they all still had guns," Louie said pointedly.

"And you could con the bullets right out of them," Alison said. "It was a stroll to the backyard compost heap, and you know it."

Louie shook his head. "You are the cheapest kid with a nickel I've ever seen," he grumbled.

"Blame it on my upbringing," Alison said. "You'll get your usual fee, by the usual channels. A pleasure doing business with you."

"Yeah, I'm sure," Louie said, gazing her direction. "How about information? You pay anything for information?"

"What kind of information?" Alison asked.

"Oh, you know," Louie said, waving a hand vaguely around. "I hear stories. Listen to rumors. That sort of thing."

"Rumors aren't usually worth much."

"The ones I listen to are," Louie assured her. "An extra five hundred?"

"One hundred."

"Three hundred."

Alison studied his face. "All right, three hundred. Let's hear it."

Louie lowered his voice. "You know that big mine explosion? The one that got both the Shamshir and Whinyard's Edge to cancel their contracts with the locals and pull out?"

"I was there when Montana blew it," Alison said dryly. "Lit up the sky for miles. You'd better have more than just a colorful commentary on the event."

"Oh, I've got more," Louie promised with a sly smile. "Turns out our boy Montana was either very, very stupid or very, very clever. When the fires finally went out and the Agri got busy clearing away the wreckage, they found what was left of the transport sitting flat-square on top of the mine shaft."

"Okay," Alison said, frowning. "So?"

"So?" Louie echoed. "Oh, come *on,* girl. You just finished playing soldier. Don't you remember *anything* about troop transport design?"

"I'm too tired for games, Louie," Alison said patiently. "Just spill it."

"Troop transports," he said, in a tone like someone lecturing a small child. "They carry soldiers into battlefields. Where people will be shooting at you. From below."

Alison frowned. "You talking about armor plating?"

"See?" Louie said, looking pleased. "You *did* learn something. Yes, I'm talking about at least twenty inches of Hy-Dense cerametal on the underside of every modern troop transport. With that model of Lynx, it's closer to thirty inches."

And then, suddenly, Alison got it. "The mine shaft didn't collapse!"

"Bingo," Louie said, looking extremely pleased with

himself. "And with the mercs already having cancelled their contracts, there's no way for them to reverse themselves and get their hooks into the locals again. Like I said: either really stupid, or really clever."

In her mind's eye, Alison could see that last look on Jack Montana's face. The look he'd been giving the Shamshir computer as he sent her back to their transport with the pilot code. "Not stupid," she murmured. "Clever."

"Whichever," Louie said. "Worth that extra three hundred?"

"I suppose," Alison said, keeping her voice casual. "I'll send a note about it."

"Yeah," Louie said. "Well, have fun with your new stuff. And let me know whenever I can be of service. Always happy to work with you."

"As long as the money's good?" Alison suggested.

"Your money's always good," Louie said with another sly smile. "See you, kiddo." Turning, he left the room.

Alison went to the door and made sure it was locked. Then she returned to the two footlockers. Ignoring her own for the moment—she knew what was in that one, after all— she knelt down beside Jack's.

So Jack Montana had pulled a fast one there at the end. On her, and on everyone else. He'd conned both sets of mercenaries into pulling out, thinking the mine they both wanted was permanently ruined, and left matters for the Agri and Parprins to work out between themselves.

Clever, all right. And it made Jack an even more interesting puzzle than she'd thought when she'd hired Louie to sneak his footlocker out of the Edge camp.

The footlocker was, of course, locked. But that wouldn't be a problem. Squeezing on the base of her left-hand forefinger, she slid out the plastic lockpick that had been surgically implanted beneath the fingernail.

She hadn't told Jack about this little gem, naturally. He would have wanted to know how a simple indentured teenager could afford this kind of high-tech gimmick, or what she would even have wanted with it in the first place. Instead, she'd spun him that bogus story about having dug her handcuffs out from under the shelving in the Shamshir storage hut.

Now, it seemed, Jack hadn't been entirely honest with her, either.

Because Alison listened to stories, too. And one of the most interesting ones recently concerned an incident a month ago aboard a liner called the *Star of Wonder*. An incident centering on a high-level power struggle between Cornelius Braxton and his board director Arthur Neverlin for control of the huge megacorporation Braxton Universis.

And right in the middle of that struggle had been a boy named Jack. A boy who was reported to have an uncle named Virgil, like the Uncle Virge Jack had called to when that spaceship had shown up and shot those Shamshir fighters off her back.

Trouble was, the name of the kid on the *Star of Wonder* hadn't been Jack Montana. It had been Jack Morgan.

Was Jack Montana really Jack Morgan? Very possibly. Maybe there would be something in his footlocker that would confirm that. Maybe there would be other interesting items, as well.

And if so, there were people out there who would pay money for that information. A great deal of money.

Slipping the tip of her lockpick into the lock, she set to work.

Timothy Zahn is the author of twenty-three original science fiction novels, including the very popular Cobra and Black-collar series. His recent novels include *Angelmass* and *Manta's Gift.* His first novel of the Dragonback series, *Dragon and Thief,* was named a Best Book for Young Adults. He has had many short works published in the major SF magazines, including "Cascade Point," which won the Hugo Award for best novella in 1984. He is also author of the bestselling *Star Wars: Heir to the Empire,* among other works. He currently resides in Oregon.